DEAD AND

BEYOND

Ancient Legends

JAYDE SCOTT

Other titles in the Ancient Legends series

A Job From Hell
Beelzebub Girl
Voodoo Kiss
Forever And Beyond
Shadow Blood

Other titles by Jayde Scott

Black Wood
Mortal Star
The Divorce Club
Born to Spy

For Foxy, Silver and Tabby

You taught me the true meaning of love …

Acknowledgments

As always, thanks goes out first to my spouse...for both being my soul mate and best friend, my brainstorming partner, and a constant encouragement. I thank God every day for bringing us together.

Thank you to my kitties, who gift me with tons of laughter and smiles each and every day.

A huge thank you goes out to my editor, Shannon, for believing in this story and the characters, and for always laughing at the right moments.

Thanks to my dear friends and fellow authors, Trish and Christine—your valuable advice and insight have helped shape this book and my writing in general.

Thank you to each and every one of my readers and fans. Without you, none of this would have been possible.

Prologue

A full-blown confrontation wasn't Gael's style. In fact, he prided himself on his talent for stakeouts; lurking in the corner, invisible to the mortal eye, stalking his victims to learn everything about them, until he could finally strike. This particular victim, however, was better protected than a queen. Certainly not his usual, easy stalk, but Gael liked a challenge. It gave winning more meaning. And Gael was a winner all the way.

He blew a gust of hot breath into his hands to keep them warm, his eyes all the while focused on the hidden entrance in the rock formation. The place was concealed by twisting pines and towering ferns, so no human would ever stumble upon it. Gael watched the thick branches stirred by the howling wind. Not only was it well hidden, it was creepy too, just like the freaky child queen herself. He let the word roll on his tongue, testing the sound of it. *Shadowland*—a hidden civilization that had been untouched by the outside world for thousands of years. It was the place where he belonged. He knew it because he had been dreaming about it for as long as he could remember. Queen Deidre resided in the mausoleum, probably feeding from her own people's life essence that very instant. He had once offered his help to save her soul from her dying body, but she had brushed him off like an annoying fly. Disrespected him. He consoled himself that he would have the last laugh eventually. Once their most precious possession was gone, so was Queen Deidre, and he would be owner of both thrones: the Shadows' and the Lore court's.

Glancing up at the inscription carved deep into the granite, he recognized the words immediately—it was an ancient language and Queen Deidre's trademark warning. Immortals knew not to cross into her territory, unless they wished to face her wrath. Well, he wasn't *any* immortal, and soon everyone would find out.

The full moon cast a glowing light on the tall trees. The cool September breeze seeped under his dark cloak and turned his skin into goose bumps. He hated how vulnerable his mortal body was and how much the Scottish weather got to him. Irritated, he wrapped his cloak tighter around him and scanned the familiar darkness for the umpteenth time, even though he knew the girl and boy wouldn't arrive for another minute or two when the turning would finally begin.

He had watched the entire procedure for days now. It always followed the same routine.

Eventually, a soft crack carried through the air and the opening in the mountain widened. The boy emerged first, followed by the girl. She was wearing the same jeans, gray top and black, hip-long jacket as the night before. Her long, jet-black hair was tied up in a ponytail, bouncing slightly as she took a tentative step forward. The soft light of the moon revealed the hesitation on her face and in her dark blue eyes.

"Angel," the boy said softly, his palm reaching out to cup her face.

She jumped a step back, as though his touch seared her skin. "No, Brendan. Nothing's changed, so don't you dare touch me."

The boy remained silent as he regarded her. A moment later, the moon broke from behind the clouds, illuminating his dark clothes and shiny hair that brushed the collar of his long coat. It was the way the Shadows dressed, the way Gael liked to dress to pretend he was one of them. The soft rays of light gave Brendan's perfect skin a bronze hue. For a moment, the boy looked like a statue, so graceful, so terribly cold. And then the changing began.

The ground shook slightly as Brendan's skin grew pallid and clammy, and a growl rose in his throat. His pupils slowly dilated before his eyelids shut. The wind began to blow harder, swaying the summer leaves in the trees. Angel flinched but didn't retreat. Brendan's face remained expressionless as he dropped to his knees and threw back his head, bursting through his clothes. His arms and legs shortened, his muscles bulged as dark fur began to sprout from his human skin. A long and painful howl rippled through his chest the same moment his face morphed into that of a large wolf with black eyes that seemed to absorb the light. Whimpering, the wolf moved closer to Angel and buried his snout into her palm, as though to smell her even though no Shadow could smell or sense another.

Angel pulled away whispering, "Go away, Brendan." With a last glance back, the wolf took off through the trees and disappeared into the night. She didn't leave straight away. She never did. It was her only chance of being alone, without the Shadows' supervision. This was his cue. He had been working on his plan for weeks; it wasn't perfect but Gael was determined to make the best of it. He had met with her for almost a week; same time, same place, never long enough to answer her questions. He had earned her trust, awakened her curiosity, and now he was about to bring his mission to a fruitful climax. One that would shake the Shadows' world.

Carefully, he straightened from his crouching position and began to move toward her. "Angel." His voice came low and soothing, supposed to instill trust and confidence in her. It was the same voice he used when talking to a child.

Angel didn't flinch when she turned to face him, which was a good sign. The girl thought herself safe.

10

They all did. He stopped a few feet away from her to give her space. It was yet another one of his strategies to make her believe his words.

"You're back," Angel whispered. In the light of the moon, she looked younger than seventeen, and certainly not strong enough to fulfill the purpose the Shadows had in store for her.

Gael smiled even though he wasn't sure she could see his face in the darkness. "I told you I'd come to get you."

Her big eyes sparkled with curiosity. "Right. But I'm not going. Not until you answer my questions." She strained to peer beneath his hood to make out his features, but he kept his head slightly bowed so the moon wouldn't reveal his identity. That part would come later.

He heaved an exaggerated sigh. "Angel, you have to trust me because I'm one of you. Or how else could I have crossed the perimeter?" His answer seemed to please her, and her stance relaxed a little.

"I don't understand this secrecy."

"Is Brendan gone?" Gael asked, ignoring her unspoken question.

She nodded. "He'll be back at sunrise."

"We need to talk," Gael said.

"You keep saying that, but you never tell me about what." Her voice still didn't convey any sort of mistrust. She most certainly thought he was one of them. He liked that.

"There's something Deidre never told you. I think it's time you knew the truth. Come, walk with me." In a bold moment of sheer folly, he reached out his hand, not really expecting her to grab it. But she did. Her fingers touched his, sending a familiar jolt of electricity down his back. His powers began to tingle beneath his skin, so exquisite, so close, and yet so far away.

"I can't walk too far. You know the rules," she said.

"Rules are meant to be broken. I promise nothing will happen to you."

She hesitated but eventually let him lead her away from the entrance. His hand clasped hers as he guided her through the trees. The clouds parted and the moon illuminated their way. He could still spy the entrance in the distance when Angel halted, and he knew that was about as far as she'd go.

"Okay," she said, pulling her hand free. "Tell me."

"It's a secret, Angel. You mustn't reveal it to anyone."

"Is that why you're not showing your face?" she asked.

"You want to see my face?" She nodded. He smiled at her childlike enthusiasm at the outlook of mystery and excitement. It probably was a welcome diversion in her otherwise dreary existence. "Promise me you won't tell anyone."

"I promise," she whispered.

Slowly, he pulled his hood back to reveal his face. She had never seen him before, but he knew she couldn't miss the resemblance, unless she didn't own a mirror.

A tiny gasp escaped her throat. Her eyes widened as she regarded his face with the same straight nose, high cheekbones and full lips. Even the eyes were alike, dark and deep, full of secrets and a past that was long erased from her memory.

"I'm your brother," he said in the most tender voice he could muster. Seconds passed by. The wind blew her hair away from her face, revealing surprise, fear, shock, and uncertainty as she tried to process the little information he just gave her.

"I thought my family was dead." Angel's voice sounded choked. He grabbed her hands, unsure how she'd react if he hugged her. He decided it wasn't worth the risk.

"That's just one of many lies Queen Deidre told you."

She shook her head. "But why would she do that? The Shadows have been nothing but kind to me."

"It's a ploy to get your cooperation, Angel. Deidre feeds on her people's life essence. Soon, she will start to feed on yours because you're strong. Your life essence will help her body heal so she can become what she once was." He drew a deep breath, preparing himself for the most important part. "Listen, I came to get you because you're not safe here. You're not safe anywhere, unless you come with me."

She didn't argue. Maybe someone had told her about Queen Deidre before. Or maybe she had found out on her own. Either way, Angel's knowledge aided his plea. Her brows drew to a frown. "How do I know you're telling me the truth about who you are?"

He had sensed she'd ask this question, so he had known to prepare. "We both carry a mark in the shape of a half moon a few inches below the right collarbone."

"Someone could've told you that."

The girl was clever, he had to admit that. "Of course. But there's something no one else knows, something you never dared to tell anyone. You have a certain reaction to touch that isn't normal. That's why you don't want your boyfriend to touch you, even though you're his bonded mate. You're scared of what you could do to him."

"How did you know that about me and Brendan?" she whispered.

"I'm your brother, remember? I'm a part of you. But you needn't worry. I'll take this secret to my grave because blood runs thicker than water."

That seemed to please her. Her lips curved into a hesitant smile only to disappear an instant later. "Why has Deidre never told me I have family?"

"Because she wants you to think you're alone. She wants you to trust them," Gael said.

She moistened her lips, her voice quivering with emotion as she tried to understand the magnitude of her situation. "I've been thinking about your words. If you're my brother, why didn't we grow up together? And how did you find me?"

"I told you, I've been searching for you my entire life. Several times I lost hope, but I never gave up. When I found out you were here, captured by the Shadows, and that your life was at stake, I had to come to your rescue. That's why I'm here, but you have to leave before it's too late."

A tear slid down her cheek. "How could they lie to me that I have no family when they knew I so desperately wished for one?"

"I know you have a lot of questions, and I promise I'll answer them all later," Gael said. "But right now we're in great danger," Gael said, slowly losing his patience. He knew the girl would start asking questions. He just never figured she wouldn't know when to stop.

Angel shook her head. "Of course. I understand. I want to learn more about my past, but I can't leave. If I leave, I'll die.

"That's another lie. You've been fed their crap long enough." He grabbed her hands and forced her to look at him. "I won't let anything happen to you, but you've got to trust me. You don't know the Shadows like I do. They're capable of anything." He could see her resolve slowly crumbling, her little mind sucking in every word of familial love and bonding that came out of his mouth. She had been abandoned at birth; it was only natural that she craved what she never had. It made her trusting, putty in his hands. "You're not dying without them. It's just a spell they put on you, making you feel faint and weak when you're away.

15

Once the spell's broken, so are their powers over you."

Angel took a deep breath. "And you know how to break the spell?"

"Yes." This part wasn't even a lie. He had researched his kind. No Shadow spell could keep someone like Angel imprisoned for life. But their mind games could. "I'll pick you up tomorrow night after Brendan's turning. Twenty-four hours should give me enough time to come up with a plan to get you out of here."

He could see a flicker of hope in her young eyes, as though her life had just received new meaning. She bobbed her head in agreement, and smiled. He smiled back as he whispered, "Promise me you won't tell anyone, otherwise we're both dead."

"I promise," she said, touching her index finger against her lips, as though to seal her words.

"I'm Gael, by the way," he said, pulling his hood deep over his face. "Come on. We've got to get you back before anyone starts missing you."

"Gael," she repeated quietly, and he knew in that instant he was about to change her life.

Chapter 1

Three Days Later

Okay, so here's the deal. When I was turned into a vampire—imagine a ritual and me, half-dying Amber Reed, dressed in my best jeans so I'd look skinny even in death; a hot vampire aka my boyfriend of a few weeks, Aidan, drinking my blood so my soul could travel to the Otherworld to find an ancient, meaning horribly old and smelly, spell book—I had no idea how much being a vampire would suck.

I won't sugar coat it. My dreadful turning probably set the foundation for my entire existence as a bloodsucker and my complete disregard of it. Of course I wished it happened on a drunken night out with the usual stranger following me home, his long coat swaying in the wind, his East European accent making me wonder whether he said 'my pretty' or maybe 'such a pity' a moment before his fangs pierced my fragile skin. And then imagine the feast—his, not mine—so graceful, so noble, so out-of-a-Dracula-movie, of which I've always been a fan. Now, that would've taught me a bit more respect of what I was because I wouldn't have heard Aidan's growling and slurping like that of a wild, starving animal. I didn't mind that he turn into an animal, in the figurative sense, when we made out. But when my life's on the line? Uh, not so much. Aidan didn't turn me; it was his brother, but it still took me a while to push that darn slurping sound out of my head when he kissed me.

So here's how I envisioned my new life as a vampire:

I turn from okayish in the looks department to stunningly beautiful like my best friend, Clare. Think porcelain skin, glossy hair, sparkling eyes, you know, the whole shebang.

Miraculously, maybe even over night, I shed ten pounds, preferably from my thighs. And I'm toned in all the right places.

My brain starts to use up its entire capacity rather than a meager ten percent so I can finally beat my brother at *Trivial Pursuit*. Given that he's actually an idiot and the moron who pushed me into this situation, that I still can't beat him isn't exactly confidence boosting.

My body finally develops some much needed gracefulness and my feet stop tripping over imaginary obstacles.

My four points weren't really too much to ask for. Sadly, I was still the same chubby klutz Amber, albeit a klutz with the ability to punch a hole into a tree.

Aidan said I'd get a few more abilities as I grew stronger, but I couldn't be sure he wasn't just saying that to make me feel better.

An initial lack of supernatural talents isn't the only reason why becoming a vampire shouldn't be advertised as being all candy and fluffy, white clouds. It had been weeks since Aidan's ex, vampire Rebecca, bit me in a lunatic revenge attack and almost drained me to death. I survived Rebecca's attack, but she marked me, binding me to her in the process. I could feel her presence around me when I paid attention to it. At times, it almost felt as though she was standing next to me, watching me, waiting for something to happen. But what? Initially, I thought she was spying on me to see how my relationship with Aidan was turning out. Now I wasn't so sure since I felt her presence strongest in Aidan's absence. I would've given almost anything to find out what that was all about. Knowing could've helped me prepare for the events that were about to unfold because I was sick and tired of bad surprises. I might have an advantage over Rebecca in that I didn't need blood to survive, but she was the stronger one. The maker was always the most powerful in a group with her blood gradually weakening as it was passed on from generation to generation. Rebecca had turned my boyfriend's brother, Kieran, and Kieran had turned me. I didn't harbor the delusion I'd win a battle, but maybe I could outsmart her. At least I could give it a try.

Apart from the constant feeling of being watched, something else was wrong. In the first two weeks after my turning, I felt no hunger or thirst. However, since entering Hell and seeing Rebecca gorge on a pour soul, a strange sense of yearning had been nagging at me, making me have all sorts of weird thoughts. Like starting to like the color red a lot when I was more the black type. Or wondering whether my mortal brother's blood might just taste as good as it smelled. I knew I should've told one of the other vampires about the sudden change going on inside me. But we had so much on our plate right now that I didn't really find the right time—or the right words. My bloodlust mortified me, so I vowed I'd talk to someone right after Cass's birthday party, which was a huge deal for her. Not only was she turning eighteen, she was finally getting her fallen angel powers, whatever those might be. And it was her last day of freedom. At the stroke of midnight, she'd be forever bound to Hell. Or until my brother married her. Knowing Dallas and his commitment phobia, I was ready to bet my meager wages on the 'forever bound to Hell' part.

So, you see, that's why being a vampire sucks. After a short period of no hunger or pain, I was slowly starting to morph into a blood-crazed lunatic, who might decide to wipe out a whole town. And if that ever happened, Aidan could just stake me in the heart because I'd never be able to live with myself knowing I had sucked dry innocent people.

I had been inspecting myself in the mirror for the last half an hour, changing in and out of clothes to find something that would suit my new paleness. And by 'paleness' I'm not talking about the usual lack of tan in winter. I mean a full blown, white as a ghost look that apparently comes with being a vampire. For a girl who likes a bit of a tan, it's kind of hard to adjust, so I applied another layer of bronzer.

"You know what you look like, right?" my boyfriend, Aidan, said from the bed.

I made a pirouette in my skimpy black dress that made my waist appear at least two inches smaller—or so I hoped. "A fashion model?"

"Uh—" Aidan hesitated "—yeah, that's exactly what I thought."

I rolled my eyes and slapped his arm at his unspoken comparison with a clown. Aidan didn't like me wearing a lot of a makeup. In fact, he didn't like me wearing anything at all. I knew because he was my bonded mate and, after a few weeks of dating, we were already so close I could sense his thoughts. The good, the bad, and the *naughty*.

"You're lucky you're tall, dark, and handsome. Otherwise, I just might be tempted to throw you out the window with my newfound strength. I've been dying to test it out," I said.

Aidan laughed. "I'm not just dating a hot chick but a dangerous one as well. Aren't I a lucky sod?"

He sure knew how to make a girl feel special. I grinned and jumped into his arms, burying my heavily painted face into his neck.

"Whoa, what are you doing?" Aidan asked, pushing me away.

"What?"

"I lost my very best housekeeper—" he coughed trying to hide his laughter "—recently. Remember?"

I didn't work for him very long, but he still poked fun at my housekeeping skills. "So?"

"So, who's going to wash my clothes now? That makeup stuff's even harder to remove than blood."

"And how exactly do you know that?" I cocked a brow and regarded him amused. He turned a very attractive shade of red.

"Let's just say, feeding from a bag of Type O blood from The Red Cross can be a bit messy when you turn into a ravenous monster."

"I wondered what that ravenous monster used to do before he went vegetarian."

"Lucky for us, the Shadow spell worked and you'll never know," Aidan muttered.

I fidgeted. I really hoped he was right because I never wanted to find out what drinking from a bag of blood feels like, let alone right from the living source. I patted his back. "I used to think someone needed a dribble bib," I said, trying to lighten up his mood. "But don't worry, your secret's safe with me."

"What secret's safe with you?" Kieran asked from the door. Aidan's gaze snapped in his brother's direction. I was still amazed how much they looked alike. If it weren't for Kieran's bulkier physique and his eyes being a slightly paler shade of blue, they could've been twins. Now, personality wise they couldn't be more different. Aidan was the responsible one while Kieran couldn't stop hitting on anything wearing a skirt—or sponging off his brother's money. Still, I liked him a lot. He was fun to be around because he understood my sense of humor. Or so he pretended. You could never be sure with Kieran.

I opened my mouth to speak when Aidan shot me a warning glare. "Don't you dare!"

"What?" I shrugged and walked over to Kieran, pretending to push him out of the room as I whispered, "Your brother knows a lot about makeup."

"You're so mean." Aidan's arms wrapped around my waist and pulled me back toward the bed. I tumbled into the sheets in a fit of giggles with Aidan on top of me. His fingers reached the ticklish spot under my armpits. I burst out in laughter. Two tears rolled down my cheeks as I draped my legs around him to stop the attack.

"Get a room!" I heard Kieran say.

"We have one. It's right here," Aidan said, nibbling my ear.

"When you come up for air, I'll be downstairs wrapping She-devil's birthday present. She won't be pleased to hear you missed her big day because you couldn't stop making out."

Aidan's tongue began to swirl up and down my neck, sending shivers down my spine. "Kieran, seriously, go to hell!" I said.

"Without you? I thought we were all going together. Don't worry, I'll wait. Just don't spend another hour putting on your makeup. Remember it's going to melt off in the 120 degrees heat."

"Come on, bro. Get out!" Aidan growled.

Kieran shook his head, grinning. "So much love's just gross. I hope it's not contagious." And then the door slammed shut and I was alone with Aidan and his hot lips searching mine. I let him draw me into a tight embrace and surrendered to his mouth. The thought that I'd indeed need to apply my makeup all over again crossed my mind, but a canoodle with Aidan was well worth going the extra mile and risking Cass's wrath in case we arrived late.

* * *

A half hour later we were finally ready to leave. Thrain, a demon and shape shifter we had grown close to in the last few weeks, picked us up in his SUV and drove us to the nearest portal through which we'd leave this world behind. We went off-road speeding over uneven terrain and into the woods with timber and rock crunching under the tires. The vehicle turned left and my head bumped into Aidan, giving me whiplash like I never experienced before. I blinked as Thrain plowed right into a shallow river. The water splashed on the windows, reminding me of a tidal wave. And I thought Kieran was a horrible driver.

Although this wasn't the first time I entered Hell, I still marveled at how fast one could move up through the different dimensions of the living, the dead, and the trapped. I wasn't sure I liked how easy it was to leave the relative safety of the physical world behind.

"You don't know what you're missing," Thrain said, probably reading my thoughts.

I slumped into Aidan's arms, ignoring the shape shifter. Hell was 'home, sweet home' for him. My first experience in Cass's world was anything but nice, what with Rebecca attacking an innocent soul and my brother dying in there.

Eventually, the air crackled from the telltale charged particles, the earth trembled beneath the tires, and then we drove through the portal. I swear my heart skipped a beat, that is, if it was still beating since I was a vampire, meaning dead and all.

I grabbed the birthday present decorated with an oversized bow and lots of pink ribbon, and exited the car. The air was too hot to breathe. Not even so much as a breeze stirred. Sweat immediately started to trickle down my back, and I realized Kieran was right. My makeup wouldn't hold in a million years. I coughed a few times to get rid of the scratching sensation in my throat and followed Thrain past the Boulders of Hell to the huge mansion in the distance.

With its dark red brick, tiny turrets and the living stone gargoyles guarding the perimeter, the house looked even scarier than I remembered it. One of the gargoyles turned its head and peered at me through glowing red eyes, making me flinch. They were butt-ugly demons that could bite one's limbs off in a heartbeat with their razor sharp. I swallowed hard and grabbed Aidan's arm for support, ready to push him in front of me in case the demon gargoyle decided to attack. Not that I didn't love my boyfriend and wouldn't miss him, but I figured he was older and probably had the vampire ability to grow back a limb. I had yet to learn how to do that.

The house was filled with people I didn't know. The previously posh interior looked like someone decided to turn it into a Barbie dollhouse with silver, handwritten happy birthday banners adorning the otherwise white walls. Red roses dipped in glitter and sparkling crystal flutes caught the light of the chandeliers. The worst, however, was the music blaring through the speakers: Stevie Wonder's *Happy Birthday* on replay.

"What's that noise?" Aidan shouted in my ear.

"It's Cass singing. What did you expect?"

I grinned and pointed at the door where Cass was just about to make her grand entrance in a shimmery, silver, floor-length gown that clashed with her red, unruly locks. As she reached us she began to sing at the top of her lungs, "And the whole day should be spent in full remembrance 'cause tomorrow I'll be bound to this shoe sole and forced into obedience. Happy Birthday to me. Happy Birthday."

I stared at her, lost for words.

"Did she just stay she'll be bound to a shoe sole?" Aidan asked.

"I think it was rat hole."

"I said shit hole." Cass took a deep gulp from the glass she was holding, the red liquid staining her lips. I could only hope it wasn't wine because, technically, she was still seventeen. "See what I'm going to be stuck with for the rest of my existence? It's like turning the clock back when I was just a kid living with my parents, except that now I'm an adult, and forced to waste my time with *him*." She pointed at the handsome guy who winked at us. He wasn't just any guy but the devil himself. It seemed Lucifer had been granted his wish and now his little daughter was running Hell.

I grabbed her in a short hug and rubbed a hand over her back to soothe her. "Awesome party, Cass." I meant every word of it because the music was slowly starting to draw me in, making me want to sing along and spin in a circle and laugh my head off playing stupid birthday games.

"I see you found the electricity socket," Kieran said, squeezing Cass's arm.

"What?" She pulled away from me and narrowed her gaze.

Kieran pointed at her hair, smirking. I wasn't sure whether to laugh because her locks did look a bit like someone gave her an electric shock, or elbow Kieran in the ribs for being an idiot and trying to ruin her day. It wasn't the poor girl's fault she lived in this relentless heat that would make straightening anyone's hair impossible.

"Did you leave your brain at the door?" Cass slapped her forehead. "Oh, wait. You couldn't have since you don't actually own one."

"That's because it had to go in search of yours to wish it a happy birthday," Kieran said, grinning.

Aidan leaned in to whisper in my ear, "Are you sure she didn't end up with the wrong guy? I could've sworn my brother and she are meant to be together."

"I know. Such a waste, huh? Imagine their weekends together." I clicked my tongue. "Domestic bliss."

"Come on, let's mingle. Maybe we'll find your brother. I need to talk to him." Aidan pulled me after him into the hallway. Even though I didn't like him telling me what to do, I gave in as I spied my friend and voodoo priestess, Sofia, in the distance. By the time we squeezed our way through the huge, crowded mansion, she had disappeared out of sight and my feet were killing me. I swear it wasn't just my fangs that grew an inch or two.

"I'm going to the restroom," I said to Aidan.

"Why? You look absolutely flawless, my love."

"Aren't you the sweetest?" I rose on my toes to give him a kiss, but barely reached his chin.

He smiled. "I don't know why you need to mess with perfection, but just hurry. I hate being alone with all these demons. And babysitting Kieran is a full time job."

The last part was definitely true, however, I couldn't help him out. If I didn't squeeze out of my high heels soon, my feet might just explode. I had to ask a few demons aka the service personnel for directions, but reached the toilet eventually. As soon as I was inside, I locked the door and kicked my high heels off. You'd think as a vampire I was way past developing blisters and blotchy skin. Fat chance.

I sat down on the toilet seat and inspected my throbbing feet. My toes were sore where the leather straps had cut in and two small blisters had already formed. Jumping on one leg, I walked over to the sink to soak a tissue in cold water, then pressed it against the wounds as I inspected my face in the mirror. In the bright light of the lamp, I realized Aidan was right. My heavy makeup did look a bit like war paint. The black eyeliner had smudged all around my eyes, and you could see every fine line, making me look way older than my eighteen years. But the light in the living room wasn't as harsh, so it probably gave me the sultry smoky eye effect I read about in Cosmo. I peered down at my tight dress, wondering why I hadn't bothered to put on seamless underwear, when something, like a dark shadow, moved across the mirror.

"What the heck?" Startled, I took a step back, only to inch forward again to inspect the smooth surface. A thin layer of charcoal gray smoke seemed to seep out

29

of the mirror and spread across the counter. I raised my hand to touch it. A warm sensation washed over me where my fingers dived in. Uneasiness settled in the pit of my stomach, but I shrugged it off. Maybe it was part of Cass's show. Or maybe she was pissed because I didn't check out her fabulous birthday cake the second I came in the door. As a fallen angel who loved chaos, she was unpredictable and hooked on drama and special effects.

"Amber." A whisper somewhere behind me. I turned my head sharply, wondering why I hadn't noticed before that someone was in the same room with me. And that's when I felt the shove, like a punch between my shoulder blades that made me lose my balance. I tumbled forward and hit the wall. Wincing, I pushed up to my feet and scanned the room. No one here. It didn't make any sense. I knew someone had hit me. I wasn't going bonkers. Then again, I was a vampire. Basically, my body was dead; maybe my brain was slowly starting to follow suit.

The fog began to shift and take shape as it inched closer. I squinted to get a better look, and for a moment, I almost thought I caught a glimpse of a woman's face. And then it dissipated again, only to gather around me, traveling up my body a moment later. Something cold touched my face. I let out a shriek. My heart began to pump harder. My hands reached up to protect my face, but it was too late. As the fog engulfed me, I could feel it inside my mouth and nose, like smoke from a fire travelling down my throat. The sensation of something burnt drove tears to my eye and made me cough. For a second, I could barely breathe, and then the air cleared and the scratchy sensation in my throat was gone.

I opened my eyes, only now realizing I must've closed them at some point. The bathroom looked just as before. Tidy. Deserted. No sign of the fog or a fire that might've caused the smoke. Squeezing back into my high heels, I moistened my wrists under the cold-water faucet to steady my racing heart, and left the bathroom in search of Aidan. The horrid *Happy Birthday* song from before had been replaced with something more modern played at a mellow volume. I found my boyfriend engrossed in conversation with voodoo priestess, Sofia.

"Amber, are you okay?" she asked, regarding me intently. Her tight dress made her look even taller than she was. Her dark hair was tied up in a ponytail and fell over her naked shoulders.

"Hey." I smiled, but my face felt frozen. "So good to see you."

Aidan frowned and inched closer until I could feel his breath on my skin. I didn't think his face could get any paler than it was already, but it did. "What's wrong with your eyes?" he asked.

My temper flared. "You don't like my makeup. I got it loud and clear. Now, get over it."

"No, that's not what I meant," Aidan said. The sharp edge in his voice made me nervous. The way they stared at me made me feel like a freak. I opened my mouth to tell him where he was going to sleep for the rest of the week when Sofia's voice rang in my ear, slow and hesitant. "Your eye color's changed."

"What?" I flicked my compact mirror out of my handbag to regard myself, and almost choked on my breath. I had always wanted to be different. Now I certainly was, whether I liked it or not.

Chapter 2

I turned my head to the side to inspect myself from all angles. My left iris had changed into a dark purple shade while the right one was a very deep red. Red and purple weren't my colors, but I had to admit my new eyes gave me an interesting flair.

"What did you do?" Aidan asked, cautiously.

Sighing, I snapped my compact mirror shut and tossed it back inside my handbag. "Seriously, Aidan, why do you always assume whatever happens has something to do with me?"

He took a deep breath. His gaze never left me as he spoke very slowly. "Because you disappeared for two minutes, and when you came back—" he pointed at my face "—need I say more"

"Maybe it's some sort of new bloodsucker ability."

He shook his head. "Did you—" His voice trailed off, but our telepathic connection finished the sentence in my head.

"Drink?" I groaned, irritated by his implication. "Of course not. You're such a moron. You know I'm not some blood-crazed monster roaming the streets at night in search of my next victim." I scoffed. "Unlike someone I know."

"Come on. That's hardly fair. It was a long time ago." He cocked a brow meaningfully. "Did someone offer? Some people would give anything to become what we are."

"Stop flattering yourself. I'm sure there's a perfectly reasonable explanation."

"Like?"

I bit my lip, deep in thought. "It's a necromancer thing."

"Yeah." He nodded, but I could tell by the frown lines on his face he wasn't convinced. Sofia shot me a hesitant smile. I ignored her as I turned to Cass and the girl heading for us. With her long, curly hair and freckled skin, she was the spitting image of Cass, but two dress and cup sizes bigger.

Cass pushed her forward, ready to start the introductions. "Patty, this is Amber, her boyfriend, Aidan. You know Soph already. Guys, this is Patricia. You can call her Patty or Muffin."

Patty laughed as she grabbed me in a tight hug as though we were already best friends.

"You're her aunt, the Seer?" I asked. "I thought you were locked up in a haunted bakery."

Patty rolled her eyes. "Yeah, I get that a lot. Followed by, why are you two the same age? What's with the extra pounds? How did you escape your prison? Let's just say, I'm on *parole*."

"The Big Boss—" Cass pointed at the ceiling "—has decided to give her the night off since our birthdays are on the same day. At the stroke of midnight she'll be whisked off in a huge pumpkin back to the Swiss Alps. Isn't that very Cinderella?"

"She made the pumpkin part up, but everything else is true." Patty spun in a circle and took a few exaggerated breaths. "That's what freedom tastes like. Me likey."

Aidan shot me an amused look. "You two could be twins, Cass."

"You should've seen us before Patty fell into the chocolate muffin dough," Cass said.

My jaw dropped. Granted, Patty was a bit chubby, but only Cass could be so blunt. Patty didn't seem to mind though. "Do you have any idea what it's like being stuck somewhere and having no one to talk to, except for a napping cat?" she asked, grinning. "Oh, wait. You will soon enough. Trust me, once you're stuck with your dad for the next fifty years or so, you can say goodbye to that waist of yours."

I peered from one to the other as I tried to make sense of their banter. Both being fallen angels, Cass's curse was similar to Patty's. Both had to find and marry their soul mates in order to be able to leave what they called their 'prisons'. Cass had found her soul mate in my brother, who wouldn't wed, dead or alive. As far as I was aware, Patty hadn't met hers yet.

"I like the weird lenses. They're mint," Cass said, pointing at my eyes.

"Who's the chick?" Kieran asked behind me a moment before his shove sent me tumbling into Aidan. I rubbed my shoulder out of habit and prepared to push him back, but his expression stopped me. He looked strange; his face was flushed, his eyes sparkled as though he was coming down with the fever or something. "I'm Kieran. You must be a hell of a thief because you stole my heart from across the room," he said to Patricia, ignoring everyone else. Even though I wasn't surprised at his blatant attempt at picking up the girl, for the first time I thought I heard a tiny tremor in his voice.

"Is he nervous?" I whispered in Aidan's ear.

"Looks like it," he replied with a frown, regarding Kieran up and down. "I think he's losing his style. I can't believe it's the same guy who told me to play hard to get when I was trying to win your heart."

"You asked your *brother* for dating advice?" Cass's hoot rang through the air. I laughed with her because it was kind of hilarious. Kieran might be hot and women threw themselves at his feet, but he couldn't keep a girlfriend if his life depended on it. And his pick up lines sucked. His worst one yet: Congratulations! You have just been voted 'Most

Beautiful Girl In This Room' and the grand prize is a night with me! That one still had me crying with laughter.

Kieran inched closer to Patricia, his arm already wrapped around her waist. The creep was obviously taking advantage of her. I would've slapped him in a heartbeat, but something stopped me. The poor girl had been locked up in a haunted bakery for two years. She was probably thankful for the bit of attention coming from a good-looking yet extremely cheesy guy. Who was I to deny her a bit of fun?

"You smell like—" Kieran took a whiff and closed his eyes as though to savor her scent.

"Dough and baking powder?" Cass prompted.

"No." He shook his head, his eyes boring into Patricia's, whose cheeks were just as flushed. "Roses and a warm summer rain." Patricia giggled. He continued unfazed by Cass's scowl, "What's the name of your perfume? Catch of the Day?"

Cass's gaze moved from Patty to Kieran and then back to Patty, her face slowly turning into a mask of fury. "No way! This isn't happening. Whoa, get him away from her. It's like watching a dog drool all over a pretty dress. Just gross."

"Did she just call me a pretty dress?" Patricia said.

Kieran laughed. "What can I say? Cass always had an amazing way with words. But she's a good friend, so she's forgiven."

"In your dreams, moron. Maybe when Hell freezes over," Cass spat.

"Come on," I said, pulling her away.

She struggled against my iron grip. "I don't want to go. He's doing that thing of his, and it's just gross. I'm not letting him bang Patty."

"No one's banging anyone," I whispered, peering at Cass's father who stood across the room, paying us no attention.

Cass looked barking mad. Luckily, she wouldn't receive her fallen angels powers for the next couple hours, or I might've needed to call in reinforcement. But even without her powers she didn't follow me out without putting up a fight.

"No, you don't understand. I can see the silver thread between them. He's her bonded mate," she hissed.

"That's just your fear talking," I said. Aidan grinned as he grabbed her other arm and helped me pull her into the hall.

"Not fear. My worst *nightmare*," Cass yelled. "I'd rather she spent her days locked up in that bakery than hook up with *him*. He's an idiot. He cannot, *must not* hang out with her."

Ignoring the party guests all around us, I forced her to look at me. "Even if it were true, you can't change it."

Her stunning green eyes widened. "Of course I can."

"No, Cass," Aidan said slowly. "You're not getting involved."

"Why not? You're just saying that because you're his brother and you want the moron to hook up with my family."

My gaze implored Aidan to tread carefully. Cass had a short temper and she never forgot. Apparently, she wasn't just anyone because even the Shadows feared her. So she had to have some major legacy up her sleeve that would surface eventually, and I didn't want her wrath unleashed on my boyfriend.

"I'm not saying that because I'm his brother. I just don't want her to hate you."

I could see Cass's mind working, weighing up possibilities. She was a clever girl; she'd do the right thing.

Her face lit up, and for a moment I really thought she came to her senses—until her lips curved into a nasty smirk. "Toss it. One day she'll thank me."

I peered at Aidan, who peered back at me, lost for words. When I turned back to Cass, she was gone.

"I have a bad feeling about this," Aidan muttered. I nodded and fell into his arms so he wouldn't notice the sudden pang of hunger washing over me. My nose picked up my brother's scent a moment before he came down the stairs, cheeks flushed, eyes sparkling now that he was back in the land of the living.

Someone growled.

"Amber?" Aidan's voice seemed to come from far away. My lips twitched. My focus sharpened on my laughing brother. He looked so young and healthy. And *alive*. I had never felt so hungry in my life.

Then that growl again. It took me a while to realize it was I who made that sound. A moment later, I pounced.

Chapter 3

Strong arms pinned me to the ground. I struggled as Aidan's voice whispered in my ear, "What's wrong with you? You almost killed your brother."

Aidan kept his strong grip on me as I sat up and peered around me. The door to the living room stood wide open. I could see Dallas inside, chatting to Cass's father.

"Are you sure? He looks pretty alive to me." I had no idea what Aidan was talking about. All I remembered was the growl, and then landing on the floor with a loud *thud.*

"Well, yeah, because I stopped you," Aidan said. His gaze wandered to my eyes and I knew he was about to return to the other topic that bothered him. "Your new eye color might take me a while to get used to."

"Get a grip. It's not like I'm some freak. I'm sure it's perfectly normal. Remember Layla? She has those weird yellow-green eyes, so it's not that strange at all."

"Let's hope you're right." He raised his brows.

"It's probably a temporary thing anyway, so stop making such a fuss because it's not a big deal, Aidan."

"And what about you wanting to attack your brother?"

I rolled my eyes at him because he was such a drama queen. The guy just didn't know when to drop a topic. "You're overreacting. I was happy to see him. Obviously, I wanted to *greet* him, not *eat* him. Do I look like a starving dog to you?"

"A few minutes ago...yes! Maybe we should get you a rabies shot." I slapped his arm as he continued, "You were acting like a mad lunatic. The only thing missing was the saliva." Grinning, he rubbed his finger over my lips. "Looking closer, I think I saw something foamy at the corner of your gorgeous mouth."

I pushed him back because I didn't like him making fun of me, but I couldn't stay miffed at him for long. He was too cute for that. "I demand an apology, or you'll be out in the dog house."

"Huh?" Being five hundred years old, he wasn't fully accustomed with the language of this century. Why did I keep forgetting that? "That's an analogy referring to the couch," I said. "You see, I can do dog jokes too."

"That's hardly fair. I couldn't bear to be away from you for one night. But you can't blame me, Amber. First the weird eyes, and now this." He held out his hand. I ignored it, only now realizing if anyone witnessed my brother's almost attack, no one intervened. "You must be tired. I'm taking you home," Aidan continued.

"I'm not going home and my eyes aren't weird!" I punched his arm and walked out the front door, determined to snub him for the rest of the night.

The evening air was stifling hot, making breathing impossible. Loud music carried over from the mansion. Tuning out, I sat on a large stone and peered at the volcanoes spitting hot lava in the distance. The red liquid rose high against the canvas of the night only to spill down the hill in a lazy stream. In spite of the horrible smell, the view relaxed me. I wondered how my life might've turned out if I didn't travel to Scotland to start my new job as Aidan's housekeeper a few weeks ago. Would I be going to college now? Maybe even have a part time job in London. I was in love with Aidan, so thinking of leading a different life didn't make any sense. But I was only eighteen. I missed being normal, doing normal things. I wanted to do something with my life, not travel around the world, visiting friends for the rest of my very long existence. I needed meaning, a purpose, something to look forward to every morning. Even though I couldn't have my old life back and college wasn't an option yet, I could make the most of my new circumstances. If only I found an occupation suitable for a vampire.

The volume of the music had dropped to a bearable level when I returned to the house, ready to discuss my new decision with Aidan. Not that I needed his approval, but I wanted his opinion and guidance, maybe even his enthusiasm. I knew he'd support my endeavors. As different as we were, Aidan would do anything to make me happy because, in the short time we'd been together, I had become an important part of his life, and vice versa.

I found him in the hall, leaning against the wall, facing the door, as though he had been waiting for me all along.

"Hey," he said, burying his hands in his pockets.

"Hey." I inched closer and wrapped my arms around him.

"I'm sorry about before."

"So am I." My lips searched his. His mouth conquered mine in a long, sweet kiss. I pulled away first.

"You know what's really hot after a fight?" he said, meaningfully.

My brows shot up. "A jog around the block followed by lots of ice cream?"

"Think more along the lines of soft sheets, rose petals and—"

"I'm not yet ready for *that* kind of action, Aidan, so stop pushing it." I turned away from his impossibly blue gaze and the way it made my heart skip a beat every time he looked at me. He was hot, no doubt about it, but I wasn't easy to get. "There's something I want to run past you," I said, grabbing his hand to pull him out into the night.

"Sure." His tone remained nonchalant with not even the tiniest bit of mistrust. He had so much faith in me, for a moment I was inclined to suggest checking us into the nearest hotel because I wanted him just as much as he wanted me. But I bit my tongue so I wouldn't blurt out an invitation. In order to sleep with him, Aidan had to be attracted to my inner being, not just my body. After a few weeks of dating, I just couldn't be sure that was the case already.

I sat down on the stairs and waited until Aidan followed suit before I shared my plans with him. "When I met you, I wanted to go to college and pursue a career."

"You know that's no longer an option, Amber. I'm sorry."

"I know that, and it's fine." I moistened my lips as my gaze trailed over the volcanoes in the distance, taking in the hot lava bursting into the air. Nature's natural fireworks. So beautiful, so deadly. "Look, I'm not like you. I can't just *exist* without a purpose. I need more in my life, something that fulfills me."

"You mean I just float through life without living it, without having a purpose? You officially sound like my brother." His tone appeared reproachful but his eyes sparkled with amusement. One of the many things I loved about Aidan was that he was never really cross with me and maintained a sense of humor in difficult situations. It made being honest and sharing my deepest feelings with him easier.

"That's not what I meant."

"I know," he said. "You need excitement. I totally get it. Being stuck with a bunch of old vampires must be as boring as dining with the old folks on a Saturday night."

His attempt at infusing humor into the situation helped me ease up a bit. "You're laughing at me."

"Not at all." His eyes sparkled again and the corners of his lips twitched.

"Whatever." I smiled. "You know how I hated being a vampire because I had no idea what I was getting myself into?" When he nodded, I continued. "I want to help others who find themselves in the same position. And I'm not talking about vampires alone. I want to give young immortals a place where they feel safe because I feel like I need to accumulate a bit of positive karma, both for us and them."

"Well, in that case I'll be sure to air the guest quarters and bring out the good silver."

I blinked, surprised. "You're okay with it?"

He wrapped his arms around me and drew me closer until his lips lingered mere inches away from mine. "Of course I am. I love you. I'd do anything to make you happy, even if it involves letting dangerous strangers into my home. I'd better get your brother to hook us up with some security cameras because I have a feeling we'll need them."

I drew back to regard him. "Thank you." I meant every word since I knew how private Aidan was. He had lived over five hundred years surrounded by only a handful of people, one of them being Kieran He had been a member of the Lore court because he enjoyed his job as a bounty hunter, but that was all the social contact he ever got. That he made an exception for me showed me how much he loved me.

"So—what exactly did you have in mind? Opening a Paranormal Anonymous place, and then what? Hold a weekly meeting where you share your experiences?" He bit his lip. I couldn't help but think he was making fun of me again.

"No." I shook my head slowly. "I want youngsters to see us as a refuge, a place where they can learn to use their powers without fear that others might take advantage of them."

"A shelter?" He cocked a brow. I grimaced. Did he have to put it like that? "Sure. As long as you don't expect me to take them out on job orientation days." I grimaced again. "No, Amber. You do your thing, but I'm not getting involved."

He kissed my cheek and turned to the backyard, signaling the conversation was over. I grabbed his arm and forced him to face me. "Why not?"

"In case you haven't noticed I'm not exactly a people person."

I threw my hands up. "Socializing doesn't require a diploma."

"It might as well."

"Must be a Scottish thing," I mumbled under my breath.

"What?"

I shrugged. "Nothing."

"Look." He squeezed a finger under my chin to force me to meet his gaze. His eyes glinted in the darkness around us. His skin seemed like alabaster, so soft and smooth, so perfect. Just like him. "It's not a *Scottish* thing. I'm just—" he paused, gathering his words "—ever since I was born, Kieran was the popular one. He got all the attention while I remained in the shadows to keep an eye on him. The one time I let Kieran persuade me to get out there and mingle, I met Rebecca and nearly lost my life."

My cheeks were on fire. I knew there was more to it; I could sense something in his thoughts and attitude. But I didn't press the issue. If Aidan wanted to tell me, he would.

"I'll be there to make sure nothing happens to you," he continued, "but don't expect me to assist you because that's not going to happen."

And then I caught something in his thoughts. It was just the briefest glimpse of a beautiful face with bronze skin and dark eyes. Blake. When Rebecca sucked Aidan's friend dry and left him to die, Aidan turned him. They had been best friends for many centuries, until Blake betrayed Aidan's trust. Even though Aidan never showed it, I knew he was upset that Blake once tried to kill me because he thought I was a liability to them all. The reason why Aidan didn't want people getting too close to him was because he didn't want to trust again. He couldn't bear having another friend betray his trust.

Chapter 4

The party was a great success. In spite of her scattered mind, Cass had been the perfect hostess. Maybe because it would be her last evening among friends and that's how it would stay for a long time. Upon leaving, I hugged her tight and promised to visit soon. For a moment, a tiny tear shimmered in her eyes, and then she just shrugged it all off the way only Cass could, as though her curse was all a big joke and it didn't really matter.

"What's with the weird eyes?" my brother asked.

"Contact lenses," I said, infusing as much cheeriness into my voice as I could because if I told him I had no idea what was happening, Dallas might just insist on dragging me to the nearest emergency room. Aidan was bad when he worried, but my brother was even worse. I faked a laugh. "I thought it'd be fun to look like some of the demons down here. No need to tell me it was a dumb idea."

"You blend right in." He let out a sigh of relief. "I'm glad they're fake. For a moment, I really thought—"

Eager to change the subject, I leaned in to whisper in his ear, even though I knew Cass could hear my thoughts. "You and Cass have a bond. You belong together. Don't punish her for who she is."

"I'm not mad she's a fallen angel," Dallas said. "I just don't appreciate her starting our relationship with a big, fat lie. Trust is earned, not a given, and even you have to admit, Cass failed at that."

"She didn't mean to deceive you," I said faintly.

My brother's expression became grim. "So what you're saying is, she didn't mean to pretend she was an ordinary human being when all along she was a fallen angel? I knew her stories were too far-fetched, but I wanted to trust her so I played along. I guess I could've just asked her if she was a supernatural. Yet I didn't, because the thing is: I wanted her to tell me herself, or at least *trust me* that I wouldn't judge her for who or what she is. But I never had the chance because her big revelation never came. What pissed me off is the fact that all the while I was down here in Hell, she thought she could get married to me without ever revealing her identity. I'm sure in her mind *none* of it was deceit. So should I be mad? I dunno. You tell me." His hazel eyes sparkled with anger.

I shrugged, unsure whether to pursue the issue or keep my mouth shut. After all, their relationship was none of my business. Ah, toss it. Isn't that what family are for, to get under your skin and irritate the crap out of you with their judgment?

"I know she lied," I said. "But everyone tells fibs every now and then. No one ever makes a big deal out of it. It's not my place to tell you what you should or shouldn't do, but you have to start seeing her point. She thought she'd lose you if she told you who she was. Now you're being a drama queen. Just be happy you still have a girlfriend. She did save your sorry ass, you know." Smiling, I patted his shoulder and turned away, leaving him to his own thoughts. I knew if I nagged him any longer we'd end up shouting at each like we always did. As much as I loved my brother, our conversations could get heated to the point of turning nasty.

"Where's Kieran?" I asked Aidan as soon as we were outside and ready to board our transportation back to the normal world.

"Cass threatened to send Hell's demons after him if he didn't stop pestering Patty, which is the worst thing she could've done because he loves a challenge. Now he's decided to accompany Patricia home." The sharp edge in Aidan's tone didn't go unnoticed. I shot him a sideway glance but his face was turned away and I didn't catch his expression. I sensed there was more to it. But I didn't press the issue because I had more important matters on my mind.

"Are you thinking about your new paranormal charity?" Aidan asked. I nodded. "Do you have a name yet? That's the first thing you'll need."

He was right. I remained silent as I watched Thrain start the engine and drive through the portal that would spit us out near Inverness. Even though we had been friends for a while now, I didn't want to talk about my affairs in front of him.

"What about Wings?" Thrain asked, glancing at me in the rearview mirror. We hit the barrier of the portal. The car jerked forward. As I looked out, I recognized the dense woods of the Scottish Highlands. The sun had set a few hours ago, giving way to complete darkness. The wet asphalt glistened from the rain.

"I was thinking more along the lines of Fangs," Aidan said, grinning.

"Just because I'm a vampire doesn't mean I want it advertised across my forehead." But I liked the idea. It was catchy and straightforward.

"Paranormal Initiation," Thrain said. "Or short, PI. Because everything's about initiation and gaining control over who you are."

"I like it." It sounded right, exactly what I had been looking for. "Did you tell him?" I whispered in Aidan's ear.

"He didn't need to," Thrain said. "Half of Hell knows after you decided to have a public conversation on the porch."

So much for keeping my plans private for a while until I figured out which direction to take. The car stopped in front of Aidan's gates.

"Cheers, mate," Aidan said, keeping the car door open for me.

"Good luck," Thrain said to me a moment before he sped off in the distance. At that time, I had no idea how much I'd actually need it.

It was the early morning hours. The sun had yet to rise; the woods were as quiet as a tomb. Hand in hand, Aidan and I trailed up the path to the imposing mansion. By the time we reached it, it was drizzling again. Opening the entrance door, I kicked off my boots and took off up the stairs to the privacy of my bedroom, knowing well Aidan would follow. I stripped off my clothes and wrapped a towel around me, then went about filling the tub with steaming water and lots of lavender-scented foam. As soon as I was soaking in the water, Aidan walked in and sat down on the edge of the tub.

"Your eyes are back to normal," he said.

"So it was just a temporary thing. What a shame. I kinda liked them." I made sure my body was entirely covered in foam before peering up at him. He was regarding me intently; his sparkling blue eyes radiated warmth and something else. *Longing.* He wanted me badly. I smiled and lifted my leg out of the water. The oil and moisture made my skin shimmer. Aidan groaned and looked away.

"What's wrong?" I whispered.

He rubbed a hand over his neck, still avoiding my gaze. "You're doing it on purpose."

I batted my eyelashes. "Huh?"

"Seducing me. Getting me all hot and worked up."

"And that's a bad thing?"

"Yes, because it takes every ounce of willpower I have to back off."

I ran my fingers up his arm. "Are you calling me a tease?"

"No, but you're driving me crazy." His spectacular eyes bore into me, making me feel as though he could see right into my soul. I pushed up on my elbows to place a soft kiss on his lips, then another and one more until his breathing quickened.

His mouth reached the spot above my collarbone and left a trail of kisses up and down my neckline. I sighed with pleasure and pulled him into the water on top of me. My hands moved beneath his shirt to help him out of his soaking clothes. Aidan placed a last kiss on my lips and pulled away. "You're not ready, Amber. Let's not do something you might feel sorry for later. Enjoy your bath. I'll be in the library." His voice was low and hoarse, filled with regret. I nodded because he was right. As much as I wanted to get intimate with him, I needed more time. But boy was it hard to keep saying 'no'.

* * *

When the water had cooled down, I stepped out of the tub and wrapped my cozy bathrobe around me to join Aidan in the library. The sun was about to rise in the distance, casting a golden hue over the backyard with its blooming rosebushes and dense shrubs. I stood near the window and peered at the stunning display of greenery stretching as far as I could see. Even though I been in Scotland for a few weeks now, I still marveled at the magical beauty of the Highlands and the clean, crisp air.

Aidan fed the blazing fire in the fireplace and joined me, wrapping his arms around me as he pulled me close. "How will you find your young immortals in need?"

"I don't know," I said. "I was hoping they would find me. Maybe I'll run an ad on *Facebook*."

He grimaced. "Unless you want the whole world to know that you're a vampire, that's not happening, babe. I know a few people in the Lore court. They could help spread the word."

"You want to go back to the Lore court?" My heart started to pump harder in my chest. I still remembered the last time he visited that godforsaken place. The current ruler, demi-goddess Layla, had tried to imprison him because he had found his mate. I managed to save him by striking a deal with the Shadows: my abilities for his life, but things didn't go according to plan. The Shadows kept me hostage and tried to mess with my mind. Layla came after me to kill me so she could have Aidan. And I ended up losing my life. I didn't want him to go back. He couldn't risk his safety for my new hobby.

"You're not going back there just to help me spread the word."

Hesitating, he averted his gaze but not quickly enough. I knew instantly that wasn't the reason why he was ready to enter the Lore court again.

"There's something else I need to do," he said. "My enemies will need to know you're immortal now and that I'm ready to defend you with my life." I could sense the emotional turmoil inside him. So many thoughts fighting against each other, drawing him in different directions. The Lore court forbade the turning of a mortal, so we had no idea where we stood. Aidan wanted to keep me away from his enemies. But he also needed to know I was safe. As a necromancer carrying the prize of traveling to the Otherworld and talking to the dead, I would never be safe from all the immortals who wanted to recover something or someone from the past. Or kill me for winning the race in the first place. Aidan wanted to show them that I was no longer the helpless eighteen-year-old mortal from London. They would still try to get what they wanted, but the revelation might just make them retreat to reconsider their steps, and that in turn would grant us enough time to find a way out of this mess.

"I'm sure you know what you're doing." I lifted my lips to meet his and closed my eyes to hide the worry in them, not about me but about the McAllister brothers who broke the Lore rules. Even if Layla was ready to forgive and forget, which I doubted, others weren't.

Chapter 5

When I finally made it to bed, it was almost midday and the sun stood high on the horizon. My whole routine of staying up all night and going to sleep when most people had lunch reminded me of my summer vacations with Dallas when we were naïve and carefree, and ignorant of the supernatural world around us. Funny how things can change in the blink of an eye.

Aidan decided not to join me, so I pulled the curtains shut and started tossing and turning under the sheets. I must've been asleep for all of five minutes when I thought I heard something: a voice calling my name. Groggily, I sat up and rubbed a hand over my eyes as I strained to listen.

"Amber." The voice was a mere whisper, too low to discern whether it was male or female.

I scanned the empty room as my heart thumped harder. Gosh, I hated being a necromancer. All the weird noises I kept hearing when no one else could, all the strange knocking in the middle of the night, and the creepy shapes I kept seeing, it drove me bonkers, not to mention scared the crap out of me. I didn't sign up for this.

"Leave me alone. I can't help you," I yelled and slumped back against the sheets, ready to get back to sleep, when I thought I heard the sound of dripping water. Had I left the facet on in the bathroom? Not only was it bad for the environment to waste water, the noise also drove me nuts. Something wet hit my forehead. I wiped the moisture away and glanced at the tiny dark drop on my fingers as a pungent smell—like damp earth and rotting garbage—assaulted my nostrils. Maybe it wasn't the bathroom tap but a leak in the ceiling? I peered up at a dark stain forming above my head and pinched my nose, forcing myself to breathe through the mouth so I wouldn't throw up as I tried to place the smell.

"Amber." The voice again, this time more impatient, filled with reproach. My heart began to race in my chest. That's when it dawned on me. Aidan had an uninvited guest.

"There's no one here," I chanted over and over again, willing myself to believe it, even though I knew I was kidding myself. To be on the safe side, I decided I might be better off with Aidan around me. He was a big guy with strong biceps and that frown of his could be quite unnerving, so I figured that might scare away the odd ghost or two. And light—I got to have lots of it because, based on my meager four-week experience, ghosts preferred nighttime and the dark morning hours, creepy haunted buildings, and even black clothes. I headed for the window to open the curtains when I noticed the stains on the walls, at first just a few dark droplets that multiplied quickly until they spread from the floor up to the ceiling. It was blood. I'd never mistake that reddish brown color. A droplet rolled down my face and into my mouth. I could taste the unmistakable metal tang...and it tasted delicious. My stomach churned, asking for more.

"Oh, shoot." I swear my heart skipped a beat or two, and I nearly fainted. "Aidan!" My shriek sounded choked. I wasn't sure it had indeed found its way out of my throat. On shaky legs, I retreated all the way to the bed, almost knocking over a chair, my gaze still focused on the wall where the blood poured down in a steady stream. My head began to spin. I had never been particularly good at dealing with fear. Combine that with the sight of a bit of blood, and I'd collapse on the floor in a messy heap.

I had to be hallucinating. There was only one way to find out. Determined to prove to myself that nothing of this was real, I walked up to the wall and ran my fingers across it. Blood dripped off my hands and pooled at my feet. I jumped a step back and wiped my hands across the front of my clothes, leaving a long red trail behind. The entire floor now looked like a sea of blood, soaking the wooden floor and the rug.

A dark, shapeless entity moved in front of my eyes. My whole body began to shake at the outlook of *seeing* a ghost. Experiencing a bit of poltergeist activity was one thing; meeting the culprit causing it was another. I couldn't handle it. I wasn't ready. Not yet. Why wouldn't spirits just leave me alone?

"Aidan!" I yelled. Where was he? We had a bond; consequently, he should feel my distress when I called him. Trust a guy to desert you when you need him the most. As the ominous entity floated toward me, all I could think of was the oldest survival strategy: get the heck out of there. And never in my life did my legs run so fast.

Eventually, after what seemed like an eternity, I reached the door. With shaking hands I turned the knob and took off down the hall, daring a last glance over my shoulder. The shape was gone, and so was the blood on the walls. What the heck? Fatigue washed over me a moment before my brain switched off. My legs gave way beneath me and I dropped to the floor, losing consciousness.

* * *

Something soft brushed my cheek. Groaning, I opened my eyes too see Aidan leaning over me.

"Wake up, sleeping beauty," he whispered, inching closer to place a soft kiss on my lips.

I pushed him away, irritated, and jumped up, only now realizing I was lying in bed with the covers barely covering my naked legs. "Where were you? I called you but you didn't respond."

He raised a brow. "I was downstairs in the library. Are you okay?"

"Not sure." Last thing I remembered was fainting near the staircase. "I think I must've passed out. Did you carry me to the bed?"

"No. I found you in your bed, asleep." A hint of worry appeared in his eyes. "Did something happen?"

I peered down at my hands. They were clean, just like my clothes and the floor. Already the whole situation felt surreal, like it never happened. Did it even take place or was my mind playing tricks on me? I wrapped my arms around him and let him pull me close. "Oh, Aidan. It was horrible. There was blood everywhere! It was on my hands, and all over the walls."

He glanced around the room. "Amber, sweetheart, there's no blood anywhere. I think you had a bad dream."

With no signs of any apparition, his explanation sounded reasonable. I felt confused, stupid, so I took a deep breath and nodded. "You're right. I think I had a nightmare."

"You haven't come to terms with your turning," Aidan said.

"Maybe." I hesitated. "What were you doing downstairs?" Mistrust gripped hold of me. Ever since my ex-boyfriend, Cameron, cheated on me, I had become suspicious of people's intentions, always wondering whether they hid something from me. The nicer they were, the more I was inclined to believe they were only treating me well because they were trying to get rid of their guilty conscience.

"Helping you out with your new charity." He grinned and held up a sheet of paper with what looked like a logo on it. I squinted to read the medieval font.

"*Paranormal Initiation*. I like it."

Aidan nodded. "Great. We could print out posters and bookmarks, and pass them around in bars where supernaturals hang out."

"You're kidding." I laughed. "You have bars for supernaturals?"

"In London." His expression turned grim. "Don't even think about asking 'cause I'm not taking you there."

I raised my brows. "Afraid I'll do a couple of shots and dance on the bar?"

"No, but you're only eighteen."

"And you don't want me compromised." I clicked my tongue. "I forgot that part."

Something crossed his face. I pushed all thoughts to the back of my mind and tried to tune in to his emotional undercurrents, but Aidan blocked me out. Whatever bothered him, he preferred to keep it to himself. I pouted, hoping he'd get the hint and spill the beans, when I thought I heard something.

Aidan's mansion was surrounded by tall gates with gold infused bars that were meant to keep out supernatural beings. I could hear dry leaves being crunched beneath heavy boots. A twig snapped in two, followed by a desperate plea. And then I sensed someone touching the bars, trying to squeeze through or maybe climb over. I could feel the magic seeping from the gates, enveloping the intruder and yet not really holding them back. Why wasn't it working? Was the intruder mortal? Had one of the villagers lost their way in the woods and was hoping to find help?

I sat up and looked at Aidan, but instead of seeing him, my vision blurred and I caught a glimpse of a mane of black hair, framing a pale face and dark eyes filled with fear. My mind recognized the girl's face immediately. It was an old friend, Angel. And then a man dressed in a dark hood appeared behind her. Her yelp startled me and broke my concentration. When the pictures appeared again, the hooded guy had one hand clamped around the girl's mouth to muffle her scream, the other wrapped around her waist to pull her through the thicket toward the waiting Sedan in the distance.

A moment later, the vehicle sped off and my vision broke. My gaze focused on Aidan. His expression had changed from concern over my wellbeing to a questioning frown. I wondered whether he had the same vision, or whether he caught a glimpse of it through my mind.

"I might be gone for a few hours," Aidan said hastily.

"What?" I waited for him to elaborate, but he didn't.

"Sorry, gotta go. I'll be back as soon as I can." Avoiding my gaze, he placed a sloppy kiss on my cheek and hurried out.

I stared at the closed door as hundreds of thoughts raced through my mind, my vision instantly forgotten. What was going on? Right from the start I had known Aidan was protective to the extent of not wanting to bother me with whatever worried him. He was heading somewhere important, and this place was probably dangerous. I had always been the prying kind so, naturally, I was going to try to find out. I flicked my phone open and speed-dialed Kieran's number. He picked up after the second ring.

"Hey. It's me. How's it going?"

"Amber." He sounded flustered, as though I was interrupting something important. I squinted, wondering why the McAllister brothers were so fond of secrets.

"I need you to do something for me." I didn't wait for his answer. "I want you to follow Aidan and tell me where he's going."

Kieran hesitated. "Why don't you just ask him?"

"Because he wouldn't tell me."

"Maybe for a good reason."

I drew a sharp breath. "Do you remember when I made a deal with the Shadows to save Aidan from Layla's clutches, after which I was kept hostage in Shadowville? You were supposed to watch me that night, but you didn't." I let my voice trail off in the hope he would get the meaning.

"Come on, Amber. That's not fair. You know I was busy planning Aidan's escape from the Lore court."

"Aidan's been peeved for ages because he doesn't believe you. I could help clarify the misunderstanding once and for all, but you need to follow him and tell me everything."

Silence fell between us. Seconds ticked by. My fingers began to drum on my thigh, waiting. Kieran resumed the conversation first. "I'm going to make sure he's okay, but I'm not sharing where he's headed." And with that he hung up.

I stared at my phone, flabbergasted. For some inexplicable reason, I honestly thought Kieran would be on my side and that he'd be easily persuaded to go against Aidan's wishes. Obviously, Kieran was more loyal than I thought.

Angry, I kicked the covers aside and jumped out of bed, ignoring the sudden sense of nausea in the pit of my stomach. I wanted to follow Aidan, but I was new at this teleporting thing. Basically, I had no idea how it worked. If I wanted to know where Aidan was, I had to follow now while the trail was still fresh, or so I figured. Damn, why didn't any of the other vampires bother to teach me the 101 of teleporting? I remembered Aidan telling me he couldn't teleport when he was too weak, but that summed up everything I knew.

Ignoring the growing edginess inside me, I stormed out of the room and down the stairs. As always, the house seemed deserted, devoid of any sign of life. I couldn't feel Aidan's presence, but I stomped into the library nonetheless, just to make sure he was indeed gone. As expected, it was empty. The countless sheets of papers covering the mahogany desk stopped me in my tracks. Aidan had left the room in disarray. Whoa. I bit my lip. Something was definitely going on because I was the messy one, not Aidan. In fact, he usually cleaned up after *me*. It must've been an emergency. But what could be so important that it won the fight against his obsessive-compulsiveness?

A pang of hunger washed over me, forcing me to bend over from the pain. Gritting my teeth, I held my breath, ready to wait it out, but it didn't subside. My gaze blurred as though I was looking through mudded glass. I rubbed a hand over my eyes and my focus returned, only to blur again. My limbs felt so weak I could barely stand up straight, let alone call for help.

"No." I shook my head at the sudden urge to *drink*. Not coffee, tea, or the bottled water that was advertised to come from a pure mountain stream in the Alps. It couldn't be happening. Kieran had turned me and, thanks to the Shadow ritual, he didn't need blood to survive, so neither should I. What was wrong with me?

My arms and neck were tingling. My clothes were drenched in sweat. I felt drained as if I had just donated half my body's blood. I didn't want to feed but the dizziness became unbearable until I thought I might just turn crazy.

I needed blood. Now. But where would I get it from? And then I remembered, before the Shadows performed the ritual that turned Aidan and Kieran into the first vampires without a need for blood, Aidan used to keep a stash hidden somewhere inside this house. If I found it, I could taste just a tiny drop—okay, make that a sip. I only needed enough to get rid of this nausea and the nagging hunger because that was all I could think of.

Like a madwoman, I dashed through the house, opening and closing cupboards, knocking on the wooden floor in the hope to find a hidden compartment, while my craving increased in intensity. By the time I reached the basement, my clothes were in a mess—my top was all creased and at least one button was missing—and I was panting like a dog. I ignored the DO NOT ENTER sign and rattled the door. It was locked.

"Come on." My foot kicked the door in fury. It didn't budge. I needed blood. Right now. If I didn't get it soon, I knew I'd do something that I might just regret later. Like teleporting to the nearest hospital for a blood infusion. Aidan might not be so keen to hear about that, so I had no other choice than to find his hidden stash. On the other hand, he hadn't been feeding for a while, meaning he might've chucked it all out, but that was a risk I had to take.

I kicked the door again, and then once more, as hard as my waning strength and weak body would allow. Gathering all my force, I gave it one last kick, breaking the door open. I flicked the lights on and dashed down the brief flight of stairs.

The room was tiny with whitewashed walls and a single light bulb hanging from a long wire in the ceiling. Apart from a heap of rusty chains, it was empty. Why would Aidan need such a strong door and lock for some chains? Frustrated, I started patting the walls in the hope I might find a hidden compartment. I knew instinctively I wouldn't find one, though I didn't give up until I checked every inch.

"Crap," I yelled, storming out again. I couldn't take the hunger any more. If I didn't find something soon, I might just—

My paranormal senses picked up a sound: leaves stirring in the garden. Without thinking, I raced up the stairs, through the hall and the kitchen on the ground floor, and yanked the back door open so hard it thudded against the wall. The glass vibrated, ready to shatter, but I didn't care as I stopped to listen and take a whiff.

The air smelled earthy, raw. And then I felt it: a pulse beating rhythmically. So steady. So strong. My legs began to move. I tore through the bushes, landing on my knees, my gaze frantically searching through the leaves until I found what I was looking for.

And then I pounced.

Chapter 6

I was vaguely aware of an ugly, slurping sound. It took me a while to realize it came from me. When I looked down, the front of my shirt was covered in blood and I was holding a tiny squirrel in my hands. The poor animal was lifeless now, its beady eyes stared up at me, wondering, fearing. *Dead.* What was happening to me? The scary part was that I felt *normal*, yet I knew I had become the monster I vowed I would never be. Would this be my fate? Stalking small animals in the forest?

Disgusted with myself, I gently sat down the animal's body somewhere under the thicket, vowing to get it a proper burial later, and got up to my knees, then bowled over to throw up. My body heaved several times, but all that came out of me was clear bile, as though my cells had already soaked up the red liquid. Could it be? I had no idea. In fact, I knew nothing about being a vampire because no one bothered to brief me in. After the ritual was performed and Kieran turned me, Aidan stopped talking about his former life as a bloodsucker. Actually, 'stopped' might just be the wrong word since it implies he ever did. Before his transformation he had been so tongue-tied, I had to *fight* for every morsel of information. I knew I wouldn't get him to talk now, but I needed some answers—and fast—before this hunger inside me got out of control. Already I felt as though I was losing the battle.

But whom could I ask?

I trudged back to the house for a thorough shower with lots of scrubbing, and then returned to the garden and sat down on the stairs, my back turned to the kitchen. In my mind, I made a list of the supernaturals I knew.

Cass was my best bet because she always seemed to know everything. But she was also the one who could never keep her mouth shut. If I wanted to shout it out to the world, Cass would be the one to contact. But I wanted to keep it a secret, so telling her wasn't an option.

I didn't know Thrain well enough.

Kieran and Aidan had fought against their hunger for centuries, but I couldn't tell them because they would freak out. They did the most stupid and reckless things when they thought me in danger, like turning all Scottish and fighting people. I had no doubt they'd start blaming the Shadows in a heartbeat. Once the McAllister brothers got mad, heads would roll. While I had no idea whether it was true, I had no intention to find out.

My brain reeled, going through every possibility over and over again. Most people I knew either weren't familiar with the paranormal world, or I couldn't tell them for one reason or another. But there was one person who helped me in the past. Granted, he also betrayed my trust, and I ended up a prisoner with no means of escape. If Aidan didn't come to my rescue, who knows where I'd be right now. This time, however, I'd make sure to read the fine print before signing any contract with a Shadow.

Getting up from the stairs, I tried to remember where I put the cell phone Devon once gave me. Not being the most organized person in the world sort of made me misplace my belongings. I climbed up the stairs to my bedroom on the first floor, and started rummaging through my possessions, tossing books and clothes aside until I had a growing heap on the carpet.

Eventually, I found the tiny, silver device at the back of my closet, pushed behind a pair of shoes I rarely wore. I didn't remember hiding it in there, but it certainly made sense. No one would ever go looking inside a closet, unless they didn't mind smelling someone's cheesy feet in the hope to find a hidden cell phone. The battery was dead and I didn't have a charger—in other words, I couldn't find it in the mess I had just caused looking for the phone. But that didn't stop me. I removed the SIM card and inserted it into my own phone. Bless whoever invented unlocked mobiles.

There was no reception inside the house, so I ventured out onto the driveway, balancing the cell phone on my palm as I watched the reception indicator. As soon as the phone hit two bars, I flicked it open and stared at it for a while, wondering whether I wasn't making a huge mistake. Trusting a Shadow was as stupid as standing near a tree in the middle of a thunderstorm and hoping one wouldn't be struck by lightning, but did I have a choice? The Shadows' ruler, Deidre, had been the one to perform Aidan and Kieran's ritual. Since it seemed to be malfunctioning, I figured I could just demand a recast of a faulty ritual and Aidan would never find out. Getting in touch with Devon was definitely worth a shot.

My finger speed-dialed a moment before I even realized what I was doing. No going back now. I held my breath as I listened to the dial tone. Someone picked up almost instantly but they didn't speak.

"Devon?" I said into the silence. My heart hammered in my chest until it was so loud I thought I might not be able to hear anything else over the noise.

"This can't be who I think it is." The male voice sounded foreign and cold.

"Surprise." I waited for him to make some lame vampire joke but he didn't.

"You're speaking to Devon."

I frowned. "Yeah, I figured that much."

"Are you sure you got the right number?" he asked.

I began to tap my fingers against my thigh because he made me nervous. As usual, I couldn't read the guy and it drove me nuts. "Pretty sure since this is the number you programmed into the phone."

"I'm surprised you still have it. What do you want, Amber?"

Granted, I didn't expect a friendly welcome but his tone was downright rude and invited me to hang up on him. I swallowed down my pride as I answered. "I need to talk."

"About what? I don't think there's anything you and I could possibly have to say to each other."

I took a deep breath to calm my nerves. When I first met Devon, he was obviously looking for more than friendship. He used his charm to make me trust him. I knew I couldn't let it happen again. But I also needed to ask a few questions. Literally. If I didn't talk to someone with a pulse soon—

I shook my head, unable to finish that thought. Let's just say, someone had to know. And preferably someone who believed me. So I decided to spill the beans, all the while ensuring I wouldn't reveal too much. I could bait him. My strategy: make him curious to reel him in until he *had* to see me, but don't make any promises. And, most importantly, don't offer anything in return. Now that part might just prove my downfall because I was always offering to do something for others, and usually ended up regretting it. "Something weird is happening to me. I feel different," I whispered.

Devon hesitated for a few seconds before replying, "You're a bloodsucker now, what did you expect?"

It wasn't my fault, I felt like saying. But I didn't. No point in arguing with him. It wouldn't change anything. "It's not that." I shook my head and moistened my lips. "Listen, I need to see you. We really need to talk."

"I don't know. I'd be breaking a lot of rules."

A dark cloud moved in front of the sun, bathing my surroundings in semi-darkness. Unpredictable changes in weather's part of the Scottish charm, but it happened so fast, a shiver ran down my spine. I could feel something in the air; something dark and foreboding, gathering around me, talking to me even though I couldn't hear a word, wanting me to do something.

"Amber?" Devon's voice jolted me out of my reverie. "Are you still there?"

I nodded, forgetting he couldn't see me. Or maybe he could. The Shadows had a reputation for hovering around Aidan's property to watch their enemies. Even though they liked to pretend they were *friends*, a silent war between the Shadows and the vampires had been raging for centuries.

"Can I see you?" I whispered, adding, "Please. For old times' sake."

Silence. Then, "Outside the gates?"

"Yes."

"I'll be there. Just be alone."

The dead line indicated the end of the call. I moistened my lips and scanned the surrounding woodlands with their dark green bushes and tall trees stretching over thousands of miles of land. Devon would come, I had no doubt about it. I just wished he could've told me *when*.

The iron-wrought gates were only a few feet away. Lowering myself to the damp ground, I pushed the phone inside my pocket, prepared to wait for as long as it'd take him to get here.

Chapter 7

Devon was trying to piss me off by keeping me waiting for almost an hour. Tapping my fingers on my thigh, I was slowly starting to get impatient and doubted he'd even bother to show up. He was such a moron, or otherwise known as the magnanimous Shadow. I still remembered the way he had spoken to me, looked at me, touched me. So calm. So superior. So *eerie*. There was a lot I didn't yet understand about his race.

I sighed and stood from the cold ground to stretch my legs. A cold wind had begun to blow through the trees, whirling the leaves around my feet. I inhaled the aroma of oncoming rain and damp wood, and wondered when my life had become so complicated. It seemed such a long time ago, but until a few weeks previously, I had actually followed a routine: wake up, eat breakfast, go to school, hurry over to my after-school part-time job, then maybe even meet a few friends in the evening to chat over a hot beverage. I had taken all those things for granted—even complained about the lack of excitement in my life—and now I had lost that bit of normalcy that had meant I was still a living and breathing being. I missed being *normal*. Being a vampire wasn't worth it, and certainly not when I sucked cute, little squirrels dry.

A twig snapped behind me, signaling someone's presence. I turned slowly and peered through the metal rods at Devon's imposing figure.

Dark hair that seemed a tad longer than the last time I saw him. Skin as smooth as alabaster stretched over high cheekbones. And then his eyes. I blinked several times as something stirred inside me: shock, fear. Had they always looked this scary?

His black gaze fell upon me, taking in my features. I brushed a stray strand of hair out of my face and rubbed my palm on my jeans to remove imaginary lint. But my own gaze remained glued to him, unwilling to show him how uncomfortable he made me feel.

"You look good given—" he started.

I cut him off, finishing for him. "That I'm a bloodsucker now. Yeah, I got that part. You look good, too, considering you're a creepy shadow who can melt in the rain. Who does that?"

"No. I was about to say, given the circumstances." He raised his brows. A glint of amusement appeared in his eyes. "And we don't melt. No idea what gave you that impression." His deep voice trailed off. I marveled at how calm and composed he seemed. It pissed me off big time because I wasn't anything like it.

"You know nothing about my circumstances." I narrowed my gaze, challenging him to disagree and be a show-off, which could only mean one thing: he knew exactly what was happening to me. But he didn't take the bait.

"You're right. I don't. To what do I owe the pleasure? You said something's wrong with you?"

"Yeah, I'm kinda jittery since I haven't had a good cup of latte macchiato in ages. Thought you might bring me one."

His lips twitched but he didn't smile. "That's a gesture of affection I reserve only for friends."

Ouch. "I thought we were friends."

He cocked his head to the side. "You ditched me the second your precious Romeo turned up whom, in case you forgot, we rescued. You didn't even have the decency to say goodbye, which stung because I thought we really shared something *special*." I opened my mouth to tell him the vampires stormed in like some kind of SWAT team and tricked me into following them when Devon cut me off, "We didn't know each other well, but there was a spark there even you can't deny. And yet you did. So, what exactly gave you the impression we were friends?"

I took a sharp breath, gathering my thoughts. "As far as I remember, you made me believe we were friends when you needed my powers. But the moment

81

you had your precious book back, you deserted me. What sort of friend does that? Never mind answering that one 'cause I'll tell you. A shitty one. In that matter you're probably right. We were never friends."

"Amber—"

"I don't want to hear it 'cause I'm only getting started! You left me on a cold stone altar with a gash on my neck, bleeding to death. How could you watch me die, Devon?" I shouted. I tried not to get emotional but it kind of bothered me because I once trusted him. He made me feel special and then threw me to the wolves. That was bound to hurt more than my escape from Shadowville aka prison. Maybe I hoped he cared about me more than he actually did.

Did I had a small crush on him and was in denial? The thought caught me by surprise. I quickly pushed it to the back of my mind and glanced at Devon. He was still staring at me. Even though his expression had softened and his eyes looked miserable, it scared the crap out of me when people kept staring like that.

"Watching you almost die was the worst pain I've ever felt in my life," he said quietly.

"Almost?" Snorting, I crossed my arms. Talking about what happened that fateful day was difficult. I felt betrayed by all. Aidan, Kieran, Cass, but most importantly Devon, because he told me the Shadows protected mortals. He guaranteed my safety. "I hate to remind you, mate, but my life kinda ended that day. My mortal one at least."

"I'm sorry, Amber." He moved and reached out, then withdrew his hand again, as though unsure how I'd react to his touch. "I should've been there for you when you needed me the most."

My gaze bore into his, and for the first time I didn't feel intimidated by his height and muscles and everything he represented. "Damn straight. If it weren't for Kieran, I'd be dead and we wouldn't even be having this conversation. Just admit I was expendable."

He shook his head, his black eyes flickering with something I couldn't place. "Don't ever say that! I fought to get to you but—" He stared at me as though he wanted to say something but decided to keep it to himself. He looked so earnest I almost believed he cared, but my heart just wouldn't buy it.

"We need to talk," I said eventually, eager to change the subject.

"You mentioned that." Apart from the tiny glint that vanished just as quickly as it appeared, I saw nothing else in his expression that would betray his thoughts. I hated that I couldn't read him. "Why don't you come out and we can sit down for a chat?"

Opening the gate would mean leaving the safety of Aidan's magic behind. "Do you think 'stupid' is my middle name? I learned my lesson the last time I was almost kidnapped by one of your kind." I waited for him to start defending his friend, Connor. He didn't. "What? You have no excuse up your sleeve? That's surprising."

"Are you lonely, Amber? Is your boyfriend not spending enough time with you?"

His tone was too sweet. Too—mocking. Maybe even a tad hopeful. I could take the bite and start raving about my relationship with Aidan, which would only lead to Devon thinking he was right. Or I could just use his own strategy of ignoring everything I didn't want to elaborate on. I bit my tongue and even managed to keep my mouth shut for a whole two seconds. And then I thought, toss it. Avoiding an argument had never been my style. My gaze narrowed as I smiled sweetly. "As a matter of fact, Devon, we're very much in love and couldn't be *happier*. But, like every normal person, we do spend a few hours a day apart, you know, just to keep the fire blazing."

"I always had the impression you guys were cold. I guess that's just a myth then." His voice dripped with sarcasm. He didn't take me seriously. I wished I had just kept my mouth shut.

I raised my chin defiantly, deciding to let his snide remark slide past. "Did you get to witness Deidre perform Kieran's ritual?"

The sudden change in topic seemed to take him by surprise. He ran a hand through his dark hair, his gaze shifted to our feet for a few seconds before focusing back on me. He was being wary again.

I rolled my eyes. "Come on. You're not exactly giving away a state secret. If you don't tell me, I'll just call Kieran." I fished out my cell phone and waved it in front of his face.

"You're right. It's not a secret I was there." His eyes sparkled as he recalled the event. I wished I could read his mind to find out what he knew.

"Do you remember Deidre saying something about the spell's effect being only temporary?" I tried to make my question sound as nonchalant as possible, but I knew he'd understand the implication.

"You mean Kieran having to fear the sun ever again?" I nodded. Devon scowled and shook his head slowly. "Not possible. Our Queen would never break her word. Is that what's bothering you? Why you called me?"

"It was a hypothetical question. The spell's still working. I was asking just in case, that's all. But what makes you so sure your Queen would never betray a vampire?"

"Unlike vampires, we live by a strict code of honor. We don't lie because our word means everything to us."

"You also don't tell the whole truth."

"Look, whatever's going on, it has nothing to do with us. I swear."

I nodded again, almost believing him. "Yeah, like I said. Nothing's going on."

"It's not about Kieran, is it?" Devon said. "It's about you. You're worried."

"What makes you say that?"

My gaze searched his. His face remained expressionless as he shrugged. "You're horrible at hiding your emotions. I can read you like an open book."

"You're crazy." I snorted.

"It's so obvious this isn't about Kieran. I've known him for centuries. If he had a problem, he would come banging on our door rather than send his brother's girlfriend to do the talking for him."

I dropped down to the ground and tucked my legs beneath me, waiting for him to do the same. He sat on the grass, our legs mere inches away, with only the metal bars between us.

"Want to tell me about it?" Devon whispered.

I smiled and shook my head. "I want to but—"

"Something's holding you back. Is it your boyfriend?"

I opened my mouth to tell him he was wrong. Aidan couldn't hold me back even if he wanted to. It was the fact that I actually cared about what Devon thought of me when I shouldn't. I didn't want him to think I had become everything he despised. "You were right about before," I said. "I was a bit lonely and needed to see another human being, even if you're not really one. And neither am I, as a matter of fact."

A smile lit up Devon's face, and for a moment I couldn't look away from his dark, mysterious gaze and the tiny dimple I had never noticed before.

"Smiling suits you. You should do it more often," I said.

"I was about to say the same thing about you," Devon whispered. "You and me sharing the same thoughts. Isn't that funny?"

"Not really." The heat rushing to my cheeks scorched my skin. I moistened my lips, wondering what I was doing here. It wasn't like me at all to flirt with the next best guy when my boyfriend wasn't around. Then again, you couldn't exactly call it *flirting*, more like friendly chitchat with a friend. Albeit a handsome one.

Something washed over me, like a dark shadow, enveloping my vision, my mind.

Amber.

It was the same ghostly voice as before, only this time I knew it was in my head because Devon didn't seem to hear it. I took a deep breath and curled my lips into a forced smile as my eyes scanned the area as calmly as possible.

Nothing there.

Kiss him.

The demand almost made me choke on my breath. This was one cheeky and probably very horny ghost. I mean, seriously, did it somehow miss the fact that I was dating a very hot vampire? Why would I want to kiss someone else?

A strong breeze ruffled my clothes, pushing me against the bars until the cold metal was pressed against my skin, making me shiver. I tried to pull away but I couldn't move from the spot.

"Why are you hugging the bars?" Devon asked.

"They're so pretty. I love them so much." I smiled through gritted teeth as I tried to pry my body away. Didn't work.

A *kiss.*

That eerie voice again. I groaned. I didn't want to kiss the guy.

"You look like you're glued to the gate. Do you need any help?" Devon smiled. At least I was being an entertaining hostess in that my visitor had a good time.

"Nah, I'm good." I pushed one last time, realizing this was one strong apparition. In fact, maybe too strong for me. Ghosts usually hover around until they no longer feel they have unfinished business to tend to. This one probably died without ever kissing a guy. It was a strange request but not too unusual. I might never get it to leave, unless I fulfilled its last wish on earth so it could pass into the light.

"Hey, there's something on your face." I waved Devon to inch closer.

"Where?" He rubbed his hand over his forehead and mouth.

I shook my head. "Nope, still there. Come here, let me get it for you." He leaned forward until his face was mere inches from the metal bars. I squeezed my fingers through. "You can come closer, you know. I won't bite." I winked. "Unless you want me to." I had no idea why I just said that. My mind must've switched off for a second. Or maybe the ghost wanted me to.

He frowned slightly but didn't comment as he leaned in until I could feel his breath on my skin. In one swift motion, my fingers wrapped around his neck and I pulled him against me, surprising him. My mouth moved fast, touching his cheek in a quick and sloppy kiss, then pulled back. My hands released their iron grip and I stopped to listen. The ghostly voice was gone, just like the strange breeze. Finally, I breathed out relieved and was even a bit proud of myself, not least because I had probably just warded off some major haunting attack.

Confusion crossed Devon's face, joined by suspicion and something else, but I didn't want to hover around so he could start his interrogation. What could I possibly say? That a ghost made me do it? "I've got to go. Aidan will be back soon," I said, jumping to my feet.

"Sure. You wouldn't want to keep him waiting," Devon whispered. I was surprised he didn't ask what the kiss was all about. Maybe he was too confused and needed time to think. I snorted to myself. Yeah, right! As if guys ever did that. Usually it was, kiss and NEXT.

"Thanks for coming. It really means a lot."

"So I figured. I might've even been able to help if you actually told me what's wrong. If you wanna talk—" His voice trailed off as his gaze brushed over me, and finally rested on my lips. I ignored the questions in his eyes. It was clear he was still thinking about our kiss.

"Yeah, I know where to find you. I might even take you up on the offer."

"You gonna be okay?" Concern mirrored in his voice. For a moment, I felt guilty because I had made him come all the way down here and now I was sending him away without telling him why I had needed to see him in the first place. Then again, he had almost guessed my reasons, so maybe I didn't need to tell him after all.

"I'll be all right. Don't worry." I studied his features—perfect just like Aidan's, and yet so different. I had always been a sucker for blue eyes, but there was something about Devon's black gaze that mesmerized me. Something that beckoned to me, challenging me, daring me to look closer. I didn't want to fall for it, but somehow I couldn't help myself. My vision blurred slightly, as though I was looking through a window splattered with raindrops. A shiver ran down my spine. A soft whisper in my head urged me to do something. Definitely a ghost again. I groaned inwardly. Seriously, this whole necromancer business was a full-time job.

"Will I see you again?" My voice came low, barely audible in my ears, and yet I knew he had heard me by the way he drew his breath.

"Do you want to?"

I nodded slowly while my brain screamed at me and my heart started to bleed. Against my better judgment I heard myself say, "Yes, I do."

Devon's smile made my heart skip a beat. "In that case, I'll see you tomorrow, same time, same place."

I thought I heard something like, "It was a nice kiss", as I walked back to the house in a daze, even floating a bit, my mind devoid of any thoughts. But I didn't turn. The thought that I didn't really want to kiss Devon consoled me for all of five seconds. And then the guilt came creeping up on me.

I had no idea what came over me, or even why I let a ghost pressure me to do it. Maybe Aidan's disappearance bothered me and I needed to take it out on him somehow. It wasn't right, but I figured Devon wasn't interested in me anyway, what with me being a bloodsucker and all, and bloodsuckers being their arch enemies. Besides, I would never leave the gates. And, last but not least, I wouldn't swap Aidan for anyone in the world. He was gorgeous, loving, generous, and perfect. We shared a bond. What else could I ask for?

Aidan wasn't back when I climbed up the stairs to my bedroom and sat down on the bed, cradling a copy of Jane Austen's *Mansfield Park* in my lap, ready to lose myself in someone else's tragedy for a change. When I finally looked up again, darkness had descended upon the Scottish Highlands, and millions of stars dotted the sky. With a sigh, I closed the book and placed it carefully on the bedside table, then went in search of Aidan. Where the hell was he? My heart thumped fast and I began to panic, even though I knew there probably was no need. He was a vampire, big and almost invincible. But only almost.

Chapter 8

It was almost midnight when I checked the clock on my nightstand. Aidan still hadn't returned from his new job and my concern was slowly growing to immeasurable heights. Several times I felt compelled to call Kieran again just to have someone reassure me Aidan was a big guy who knew what he was doing. The trouble with men, however, is that their ego often exceeds their height—or abilities. Whatever Aidan's job involved, I knew he'd jump in with both feet, probably head first, to get it done. While I liked his enthusiasm when we were alone, I wasn't so keen on his attitude toward fulfilling his duties, especially not when taking risks was part of the job description.

Rubbing my eyes to get rid of the throbbing sensation inside my head, I tossed the book on the already overcrowded bedside table and decided to search for another activity to kill time. Ever since coming here, I had even developed a bit of a fondness for cleaning, probably because I was mostly bored out of my mind. Gathering the laundry, I climbed down the staircase to the basement when I realized I had completely forgotten about the kicked-in door. Leaving it hanging off its hinges wasn't an option because Aidan was bound to find out and ask questions. But I knew nothing about DIY work. I briefly considered calling Kieran to ask for help, then decided against it since I figured he was probably even more clueless than I was.

I tapped my fingers against the doorframe, begging my immortal mind to come up with a brilliant plan, when I felt a sense of urgency a moment before the unnerving sound of someone rattling the gates echoed in my ears. It sounded as though someone was trying to get in, but this time I knew it wasn't just in my head. My temper flared. Seriously, not again. I was so sick and tired of the spirit's mind games.

"Go away," I hissed.

The sound continued and pictures began to flood my mind. A dark shape hovering outside the gates, his hood covering his face so I couldn't make out his features. I realized this wasn't an apparition but a vision, just like the one I had about Angel.

Whoever was out there probably knew Aidan wasn't home and wanted to take advantage of the situation. Well, that wasn't happening. Adrenaline began to rush through my veins, making me excited to go out there and defend my home, my territory, and one of my BFFs. Forgetting all about the door, I dashed up the stairs and out the front door with supernatural speed, almost as fast as the other vampires traveled, and reached the gates in less than two seconds. My lips curled into a snarl, my fangs lengthened, ready to defend the house by shredding the intruder into smithereens.

The telltale scent of a Shadow hit my nostrils. They all smelled similar, a bit of fire and dry earth washed away by an angry summer storm, tough different in nuances. I had met my fair share of them, but I couldn't remember this guy. His body was hidden beneath a black cape, his face obscured by a hood, but I didn't fail to register his broad shoulders and strong hands clasping the bars. Red, sore wounds, like deep blisters, had formed where he touched the magic infused metal. It looked painful, but he didn't seem to mind.

"Piss off, mate, or I swear I'll kill you," I hissed. My voice sounded resolute, menacing. Inside, however, I prayed I wouldn't have to carry out my threat because I figured, vampire or not, I was more civilized than that. Killing was Aidan and Blake's thing. Kieran and I preferred to step back and sort out our differences at the local pub, musing over a pint, rather than kick someone's face in.

"My name's Brendan. I'm sorry to bother you. I wouldn't do it if I didn't need your help." He had an air of regency about him, as though he wasn't just any Shadow, but it was the guy's voice that surprised me.

Not only was he extremely polite for a Shadow, he also sounded much younger than I anticipated. Maybe twenty or twenty-five. But since they all seemed so young, I figured he might as well be two hundred plus.

"My help?" I rolled my eyes. "Yeah, heard that one before. Didn't turn out so well for me."

"Please, just listen," he said, throwing his hood back to reveal his face. I stared at his youthful features and the black eyes that were so common among Shadows, trying to remember whether I had seen him before. His face was smooth as marble with perfect skin a tad darker than Devon's, but prominent cheekbones and a strong jaw. For a moment, the usual Shadow pride shined in his eyes, giving way to worry and fear. I couldn't remember having ever met him, but something must've happened, or why else would he be here? I cleared my throat.

"Did Devon send you?"

Brendan shook his head. "No, my blood brother doesn't know I'm here and I'd rather it stayed that way."

"Why?"

"Because he's already worried enough as things stand. I wouldn't want to burden him with—" He stopped abruptly, his gaze swept away from me as he scanned the fallen leaves scattered across the ground beneath our feet.

I raised my brows. "You wouldn't want to burden him with what?"

"Never mind. It's not important."

I nodded, not quite comprehending his words because my mind still circled around his casually dropped statement. "You said he's your brother?" What did it matter whether he was? I knew I wouldn't be trying to impress Devon's family any time soon, and yet my heartbeat picked up in speed.

"*Blood* brothers," Brendan explained. "He saved my life once."

"Right." I waited for him to elaborate on his strange connection to Devon or why he was here, but he kept quiet. The way his eyes moved back and forth told me he had come in haste and hadn't prepared his speech. I gathered I could wait for him to start speaking and maybe end up wasting my whole day, or I could do what came naturally to me anyway. Interrogate.

With a big sigh, I curled my lips into a fake smile. "Okay, Brendan. You're obviously in some sort of trouble, so you've decided to ask a vampire for help. And not a strong and experienced vampire either, but a newbie who is fumbling around in the dark trying to figure out this whole supernatural world for the very first time. That's rather strange. Don't you think?"

"I know but you're my last resort."

"Whatever's going on, your vote of confidence in me is overwhelming," I said with a smirk. "We get to play friends while you need me. Once my deed's done we get to go back to your race despising the very ground I walk on."

His black eyes sparkled with passion. "The Shadows have every right to hate the vampires. You've yet to know what they've done to us in the past. Maybe you should read up."

"Yeah." I nodded. "I'd love to. Have any supernatural history books handy?"

"They're out there, Amber. Ask around. Better yet, check out your boyfriend's library. It'd shed some light on my point of view."

Why was everyone so hell bent on holding a grudge for centuries? What happened to solving one's issues over a good cuppa and parting ways with a good ole' handshake? "I think I can fill in the blanks," I muttered. "They did some terrible things to you and you'll never forgive them. But I'm sure you weren't the victims here. I can only imagine the unspeakable things you did to them to make them retaliate in that manner."

"I was never part of that."

"Really? Because you're different?"

"As a matter of fact, I am. I don't hate my enemies." The flicker in his black eyes told a different story though. Ever since my turning we were foes. Anything else was just pretense.

I crossed my arms over my chest and regarded him coolly. I know I should've asked what made him different, but this meeting was bizarre enough already. A Shadow's visit was the last thing I expected. Time to cut to the chase. "Just tell me why you're here, Brendan. We haven't got all day."

A headache began to throb at the back of my head and a sense of imminent sickness weighed me down. It was only a matter of time until I'd turn all blood crazed again. The slightest pangs of hunger were already stabbing me, reminding me I hadn't fed on the real thing. And the real thing was standing right in front of me, with deliciously sweet blood running through his veins. If he didn't spill the beans soon, I wouldn't be surprised to see a roast chicken standing there instead of him, or whatever vampires fantasized about.

Brendan's gaze focused on me as he took a long breath. "I know you met Angel during your stay with us." He said the last part like I had a choice. Truth be told, I had been sort of tricked into entering Shadowland, upon which Aidan had to get me outta there, otherwise I would've ended up with twenty to life. Almost freezing to death in a secluded mountain with a creepy child queen aka The Exorcist Kid, trapped between life and death, spinning her dark magic on me wasn't my idea of a 'stay'. I bit my tongue hard to keep back a remark, and nodded to let him know I remembered Angel, the raven-haired girl who, at that time, was the only other mortal to ever enter Shadow territory.

"I'm here because, in a way, she told me to come if something happened," Brendan continued.

"I don't understand. Does she need help? Why didn't she just get in touch with me?"

"Maybe she tried but couldn't reach you?"

"No." I shook my head, confused. "Unless—" I sucked in my breath as realization struck me. "The bars." I pointed at the gate, where his hands touched the gold-infused bars that were supposed to keep away intruders.

"She's in big trouble," Brendan said.

And then it all came back to me. "I thought I had a vision of her rattling the gates a few days ago. I didn't pay it any attention because I never had a vision before and she was being chased right before somebody dragged her into a black Sedan. What are the odds of that?" I tried to laugh it all off but the sound remained trapped in my throat.

His eyes grew wide. "Did you get a look at her attacker?"

I shook my head as I tried to remember. "No, it happened so fast. It was like a blur. I even came out and checked the gates but there was no sign of her so I thought I'd imagined the entire thing."

"Did you get the license registration number?" Excitement flickered in his eyes only to die down when he caught the expression on my face.

"It was just a silly fabrication of my mind, Brendan. I'm a newbie, so you can't rely on me for information."

"Obviously you know more than we do. We've no idea where she could be," he said.

"Maybe she had enough of you creeps, packed her bags and took the nearest exit. You can't blame her. What seventeen-year-old would rather spend her days trapped in a mountain than partying with her friends, or shopping? Last time we talked she kinda missed that."

He shook his head. "No, you don't understand! Something must've happened to her. She'd never leave without me because I'm her bonded mate."

I let out a sigh, realizing the magnitude of his words. The fact that they shared a bond explained his worry. Bonds were spun by Fate, eternal. They changed everything. I regarded Brendan intently, only now noticing that his dark eyes were blood shot, as though he hadn't slept in days. His hands were still clasped around the metal bars, and painful blisters had formed on his skin. It was as if he tried to wear a mask to disguise the pain, but I could see right through it into his raw grief. I actually felt bad for him because I couldn't imagine living without Aidan. I thought I lost him once when Layla imprisoned him, which turned me into a total train wreck. So I understood what Brendan was going through. And I liked Angel. Usually, I wouldn't spill out a friend's secrets, but I believed Brendan and I figured my words might just trigger some repressed memory or knowledge in him that could help find her.

"I remember something about a boyfriend and that she hated him." I tapped a finger against my lips as I tried to recall my three meetings with Angel and her exact words. "Maybe it wasn't so much hate as—"

"Contempt?" He snorted. "Sounds about right. I got that a lot from her."

"Why? Shouldn't she be in love with you since you have a bond and all?" It was the way the bond worked with Aidan and me, with my brother and Cass, and so forth.

"That's right," Brendan said. "She was very careful with her emotions. I sensed she was hiding something from me but I couldn't get it out of her. But none of that matters now. The only thing I care about is finding her and bringing her home safe. You've got to help me. I can't do it on my own."

I peered at him intently, searching his features for any signs that he was lying. Granted, the Shadows didn't have Thrain's tracking skills, nor were they kickass bounty hunters like Aidan, but why couldn't they track down a girl's whereabouts? They sure had no problem following me around when I was still mortal. "Why's that? Do your sniffer dogs have a blocked nose?"

"We can't find her because she's half Shadow, and we don't sense our own people," Brendan said coolly.

I stared at him blankly. "What did you just say?"

"What?"

"Angel's half Shadow?"

He nodded. "Yes."

"You've got to be freaking kidding me." I slapped my forehead. "She thought she was mortal. You know what, you people are unbelievable. How could you hide something like that from her?"

"We don't have time to discuss her lineage right now," Brendan said.

My mind was still processing the previous piece of information. Angel was half Shadow. Made sense. I clicked my tongue, thinking, and pulled my sweater tighter around me, but not because of the cold. I could sense an opportunity here. Join their search for Angel, and in return have them look into why the spell on Kieran's blood was starting to lose its effect on me. It was a simple bargain, and I was ready to dive right in. Again. Only, this time I'd make sure to read the fine print before signing the dotted line.

But even if he refused the deal, I'd still help because Angel was my friend. Besides, I knew what it felt like to be kidnapped and torn away from everything you know and love. I'd bring her home, hell or high water, because that's what friends do. Yeah, I'd show Devon that I could help a Shadow in need, even though I was the archenemy. No one was going to label me a 'shitty' friend. That title was reserved strictly for him.

"Okay, I'll do it, but I want something in return," I said.

Brendan nodded slowly as he regarded me through those black, bottomless eyes. "I'll get Devon to find out what the deal is with your sudden thirst. Is that good enough?"

"How do you know about it?" Suspicion crawled into my voice. He couldn't possibly know about my situation unless it was all planned right from the beginning.

"I saw you." He averted his gaze, muttering under his breath, "With that squirrel."

My cheeks burned. Oh, gosh, somebody had witnessed one of my most embarrassing moments ever: killing off the wildlife on the property. I was the lunatic who whacked a poor, helpless, little animal. No wonder he ran the other way instead of talking to me. I wouldn't have wanted to meet me either. Hopefully, he didn't record the entire episode on his phone and post it on *YouTube*.

"Yeah, that wasn't my most glorious moment, was it?" My laughter sounded forced. Choked.

"So, we have a deal?" Brendan held out his hand as though to squeeze it through the metal bars. I peered at the raw blisters, but didn't touch his skin in case he put some spell on me. Granted, I sounded a bit superstitious but I knew next to nothing about the Shadows and their abilities. Better be safe than sorry.

Brendan pulled back, unfazed.

"I'll need details," I said. "Where did you last see her? What was she wearing? Did she behave suspiciously before walking out on you?"

"I told you she didn't walk out on me," he said through clenched teeth. A menacing glint appeared in his eyes. Whoa, I could sense a short temper there. "The night before she disappeared, she was wearing jeans and a black shirt. We were still together at sunset. She watched me—" he hesitated, choosing his words carefully "—trot off into the forest under the light of a full moon to run some errands."

I raised my brows. "At night?"

"I'm not at liberty to discuss my duties with you. Let's just say, she likes to spend a bit of time outside before returning to the safety of our fortress, so no one grew suspicious when she didn't return immediately. After ten minutes, the guard became nervous and left his post to get her, but she was already gone and we couldn't find any trace of her."

Foul play. I could smell it from a mile. No one disappeared without a trace, unless magic was involved—or a portal to another world was opened. As far as I knew, Cass was the only person who could do that. But she was eighteen now, and stuck in Hell with my brother by her side. She could no longer leave the place to cause trouble. Unless Dallas had finally decided to marry her, which I doubted because I would've known by now. Cass would never be able to keep that little secret to herself for longer than five minutes.

"That's all you've got for me?" I drew a long breath and let it out slowly. "You know, I might be able to get more clues from *Google*."

"Figured that much." He pushed his hand into his pocket to retrieve a torn out paper with frayed edges, and dropped it through the bars. I caught it in mid-air before the wind blew it away. "This is my number. If you find anything, call me. And one more thing."

I raised my brows. "A surprise hint?"

"I told you everything I knew. I'm just as lost as you are." He held my gaze for a moment as he leaned forward to whisper, "Devon doesn't need to know."

"Right." Did I need to know why not? My curiosity was killing me, but I figured I'd ask next time because the hunger inside me had grown to unbearable heights. Getting rid of it before Aidan arrived back home was my top priority now. "We good?" I smiled at Brendan.

"Yes." He returned the smile, and for a moment a glint appeared in his eyes again, though this time it was warm and friendly and—

Blood. I blinked as I stared at the red liquid pouring down on us in huge drops, bathing his black hair and soft skin in a red hue. I swallowed hard to get rid of the bile rising in my throat.

"Are you okay?" Brendan asked, frowning. The red liquid seeped into his mouth and trickled over his pearl white teeth. I could see it gathering at the corners of his lips; I could taste its salty tang on my tongue.

"I've got to go." Turning my back on him, I ran up the alley to the house and slammed the door behind me. Only when I reached the kitchen did I stop in my tracks and raised my wrist to my mouth. Not really knowing what I was doing, I bore my fangs into my fragile skin and began to draw blood, at first tiny droplets that soon became a steady stream. It wasn't right, but I couldn't help it. If I didn't feed from myself, I might end up picking someone who

106

wouldn't survive the deadly attack of a newly turned vampire.

Chapter 9

My blood rushed through my veins, sending shivers of pleasure down my spine. Swirling my tongue, I licked the two punctures on my wrist and opened my eyes. The sun hid behind dark rain clouds bathing the kitchen in semi-darkness. As a vampire, my vision was already sharper than any mortal's, but it seemed different now. The air particles seemed to have taken on a glowing hue; the edges of the kitchen counters appeared more pronounced. I could almost see their depth, as though they had another dimension to them. Tilting my head, I focused my gaze on an empty glass of water, and then dropped it to the floor, only to catch it in mid air before it could shatter into thousands of pieces. I tried the trick once more, marveling at my heightened reflexes. Did Aidan really prefer to renounce his abilities than drink blood? I scoffed. Who in their right mind would do that?

When he first revealed his true nature, I had been appalled and disgusted. And now here I was, unable to control my thoughts that told me he was stupid for making such a sacrifice. When did I change? When had I become this monster?

I only now felt the weight of what I just did: attack myself so I wouldn't attack an innocent. What was wrong with me? Why was this happening to me, and not to Aidan or Kieran? It didn't make any sense. And yet my brain knew the answer. Aidan and Kieran had experienced the Shadow ritual first hand. To me, the spell was passed on through Kieran's blood. There was my answer, which inevitably led to yet another question: how could I get rid of this all-consuming hunger and get back to normal?

Maybe I could persuade Devon to perform another ritual before Aidan found out I was no longer the vegetarian he thought me to be. As much as I wanted honesty between us, I knew I wouldn't be able to see the disappointment in Aidan's eyes. He'd probably stand by me no matter what, but he might lose interest along the way, which would destroy our relationship. I couldn't bear the idea of losing him, but I didn't want to lie to him either.

My head was spinning. Not only did I not know whether to tell Aidan about my predicament, I also had the problem of Angel's disappearance. In my vision I witnessed her kidnapping as she pounded on the outside gates crying out for help, but it could also be just a figment of my imagination because I'd never had a vision before. I mean, dead people always seemed to reach out to me, but not living ones—and Angel was definitely alive, wasn't she? She had to be because if she weren't Brendan, as her mate, would've felt her passing and told me. I heaved a big sigh as I brushed a hand over my face, realizing I had so little to go on, I had no idea where to even begin.

"Amber? Are you here?"

Aidan's voice cut through the silence, startling me. I had been so engrossed in my thoughts I didn't hear his soft footsteps in the hall just outside the kitchen. Pulling my sleeve over my wrist to hide the now fading punctures, I cleared my throat and plastered a fake smile on my lips, then opened the door and almost bumped into him. He wrapped his arm around my waist to steady me, a lazy grin playing on his gorgeous lips. "Whoa, are you okay?"

"Yeah." My breath caught in my throat as I peered at his black hair still damp from a shower and the way his white shirt stretched over his broad chest, accentuating his ripped torso. The guy belonged on the cover of a magazine, right below the title 'Smoldering hot, and just as dangerous'.

"I missed you." His mouth pressed against mine in a heated kiss. I parted my lips and caved into his embrace, my body melting into his. His tongue found his way into my mouth, pushing slightly, swirling, and then pulling back. A soft moan escaped my throat as my legs gave way beneath me. Thankfully, he was there to hold me. Our kiss ended too quickly.

Disappointed, I peered into his blue eyes sparkling with the usual hungry flicker, questioning me, begging me to take the next step. I couldn't blame him. He had waited for weeks, mostly patiently, but there was no doubt he'd jump at the opportunity to bed me.

"You've been gone for a while," I said, pulling him into the library and closing the door behind us.

Aidan slumped on the couch with a sigh and pulled me onto his lap. I nestled against his chest and raised my lips to his neck to caress the soft spot below his ear, right where the blood pumped the hardest.

"I'm sorry. I didn't realize it'd take this long. Hope you got some rest."

I snorted. "Fat chance."

"You look glowing." His fingers trailed up my arm to cup my face. "In fact, you've never looked more refreshed."

That's because my diet took a drastic change. Maybe I should get a membership at the local blood bank. It might be expensive but better than munching on the wildlife...or myself. Now, *that* was eternal embarrassment.

"Thanks." I smiled as another pang of guilt surged through me. Now was the time to share my predicament with him and let him take charge. But I couldn't spoil the moment. In a house full of vampires with fallen angels, demons and what else not popping in whenever it suited them, moments alone with my boyfriend were rare. I felt our circumstances were slowly taking their toll on us, so we really needed the few occasions of bonding time.

Okay, I admit I was a chicken, but I couldn't bring myself to tell him. Not when he smelled so good.

Aidan moaned against my temple. "Can you do that again?"

My lips moved down his neck to his collarbone and then up, leaving a wet trail behind. I felt him shiver beneath me, and smiled as my mouth searched his again. He relaxed in my arms, so I figured it was time to start the interrogation.

"Where were you?" I whispered as I inhaled the strange scent wafting from him. It wasn't unpleasant, just...different, scary but also sexy. Like nothing I had ever smelled before.

"I told you a new job came up." He tensed but didn't pull away.

"I can smell something on you. Five layers of shower gel won't get rid of it."

He got up and reached the window in a few long strides. His broad back was turned on me, but I could sense his frown and that he fought with himself. He considered lying his way out of this, then decided against it. Due to our bond, I could read his emotions. That he hadn't noticed the changes in me told me he had a lot on his plate.

I joined him at the window and wrapped my arms around his waist, resting my chin against his back. He felt so strong, so...home. I breathed in his manly scent and knew I wanted him more than I had ever wanted any other guy. No other man would ever measure up to him. No one else would ever make me feel this way, all fluffy clouds and pretty butterflies.

"You forget I'm almost as powerful as you are now, so there's no need to protect me. Whatever this job entails, share it with me, Aidan. I'm so ready to join your life," I whispered.

He drew a sharp breath. His muscles tensed against my chin. I ran a hand down his back, mesmerized by how smooth and strong he felt. My mouth went dry at the thought of kissing him while my hands explored his body, something I hadn't done yet. I had delayed it because I couldn't cope with becoming a vampire, thinking that was about the worst that could happen to me. Well, I had just experienced first hand that things can always take another turn downhill. Call me superstitious, but I could feel the figurative Damocles sword dangling over my head. Time to take our intimacy to the next level before I completely spiraled out of control and it was too late.

"Layla summoned me," Aidan said eventually.

I blinked. "Layla? The crazy goddess chick that tried to kill me because she couldn't take the competition? Why would you agree to see her?"

"Because—" He cleared his throat and turned to face me, his hands resting on my shoulders. "I want to have a normal life with you. I want you to be safe and do all the things you want to do without anything to fear."

"So, what is it that you're supposed to do for her? Hand over your first born child?" I tried to keep my voice nonchalant, as though it wasn't a big deal, but it was. A pang of jealousy hit me and bile rose in my throat. Layla was stunning with glossy hair, gorgeous legs and the one part no man would ever dismiss: big boobs that always seemed to spill out of her skimpy nightgown she called a dress. How could I win against that? I trusted Aidan, I really did. But I didn't trust a succubus demi-goddess, and particularly not one who had the hots for my boyfriend and kept throwing herself at him.

"She wants me to find someone," Aidan said.

"Who?"

"Do you know what's kept me alive all these centuries?"

"I can only begin to guess," I said sarcastically.

"Trust. In the immortal world *my word* means everything. It could mean the difference between life and death." Aidan's eyes shimmered with pride. I figured it was yet another Scottish thing.

"So, you're saying it'd be unprofessional to tell me?"

Aidan nodded. "That's exactly what I'm telling you."

'Confidential' wasn't usually a word that featured in my relationship vocabulary. I squinted at him, ready to invade his mind and search for an answer, then decided to give him one last chance to spill the beans, after which I'd do what every jealous girlfriend with a bit of a backbone would do: start *Operation Spying On The Guy*.

"What she doesn't know—you fill in the blanks." My lips curled into a mischievous smile. He hesitated; his gaze swept across the carpet as though the answer might just magically appear. When he lifted his head again, I could see I had lost the battle.

"I'm sorry, babe. It'd be unprofessional."

I wanted to scream at him that Layla had been unprofessional as well when she sent her most poisonous snakes after me. The bites would've killed me if Aidan didn't suck out the venom. I still had a snake phobia and couldn't even watch those slimy creatures on TV without experiencing a full-blown panic attack that left me unable to sleep for days. I didn't want her to spend time with him. Not when I knew she'd be all over him whenever the chance presented itself, and knowing Layla, she always found an opportunity to get all touchy-feely. Besides, I had a right to know what we were up against. How could I protect myself when I had no idea what was going on?

"Did you get any work done?" Aidan said, changing the subject. He always did that. It had worked in the past because I couldn't be bothered to pursue the matter, but he wouldn't get away with it today. Tossing my hair over my shoulder, I shot him a venomous look and marched out of the library, ignoring his surprised expression.

I almost reached the stairs when his hand clasped my upper arm, forcing me to stop in my stride. "Go away," I hissed.

"Amber, you've been in this world for less than a few weeks. There are things you don't understand—"

I turned to face him, my eyes throwing daggers. "Yeah, because you won't tell me! You keep me in the dark like some delicate flower. And I'm not. I died for you. I gave up everything—my life, my friends, my parents, my career." I knew I was putting on the guilt, but I had no idea how else to get him to stop being so overprotective. "Can a delicate flower enter the Otherworld, obtain an ancient book, and live? No, it'd wither and die. But I came out stronger because I'm made of harder stuff than you think. Heck, I'd even describe myself as a survivor."

"You're pissed and I understand." He took a deep breath, signaling me he didn't understand a word I said. "But you're going to have to trust me."

"Why? Because you've got hundreds of years of experience with your supernatural world?" I snorted. "Yeah, right!"

"Yes, Amber. That's exactly why. You have so much to learn."

"Then teach me, Aidan." I inched forward and jammed my finger into his hard chest. He didn't even flinch. "It's like you keep me in this ivory tower trying to protect me. After everything I've been through I can handle whatever you have to say because I'm a *vampire.* There, I said it. I am what you are so I have every right to know about this world."

"Please, Amber," Aidan said softly. I shook my head as I watched his resolve crumble. He sighed and the hall fell silent. I could hear the grandfather clock ticking in the library, and started counting. I barely reached ten when Aidan resumed the conversation. "You're a big part of my life and I don't want to hide anything from you. Lying can destroy a relationship and that's why I think I need to tell you what's going on." I cringed at his choice of words, feeling bad. I wasn't lying to him, just keeping a few secrets I shouldn't keep. But the thought didn't help get rid of my guilty conscience. "For your safety, you need to promise me not to tell anyone," Aidan continued.

"Who would I tell? Just look around you." I pointed down the empty hall.

"Sit down first. This could take a while." He grabbed my hand and pulled me back into the library, then closed the door behind us. I sat down on the sofa and waited for him to join me, but he preferred to stand.

"You know Layla's a goddess, right?" Aidan began. I nodded, so he continued, "Her mother, Dara, was one of the best Lore Court rulers the paranormal world ever had. She was kind, strong, and caring. But she also had a few skeletons hiding in her closet."

"Who doesn't have a few of those?" I shot him a look. Yeah, Aidan had *lots* of skeletons in his closet. He didn't even have room to talk. And neither did I.

He ignored my comment. "It seems Dara had a few vices, and one of those was her inability to resist the advances of men. Layla always knew she would inherit her mother's throne as the Queen of the Lore court— until she found out her mother had strayed, bearing several children with different fathers."

"So she has a few half-siblings, what's the big deal?" I rolled my eyes. "Is she scared of not being the center of attention any more? That everyone might just stop talking about her for a moment at the yearly Christmas dinner?"

Aidan smiled. "Not quite, babe. Layla was scared she might lose the throne, so she got rid of her half-siblings, but she didn't move fast enough. Dara saved one son, Seth, and managed to hide his identity until it was too late. Seth's now a frequent visitor of the Lore court and Layla's most dangerous competitor for the throne. Under her mother's protection, he was untouchable. Since Dara's weak and retired, he's no longer invincible."

"Neither's Layla," I said dryly.

"Exactly. Layla thinks her half-brother has been planning her demise for ages with the difference that he kept a close eye on her for years and knows her every weakness."

"She wants you to find him so she can kill him. I don't like that, Aidan."

Something sparkled in his blue eyes. "You're way off track. And good thing too. Do you know how hard it is to kill a demi-deity? She wants him to sign a pact because she fears for her safety and throne. You see, Seth's father was a Shadow."

"Sounds like a pact with the devil. I'd run as far away from her as possible." I raised my brows, not really understanding where he was heading with this. "So what does all of this mean?"

Aidan inched closer to whisper in my ear, "The supernatural world is split into three courts: the vampires, the Shadows and the Lore court, which is ruled by a deity. A Shadow is granted his power rather than be born with it. Seth is already a deity, and now he's looking for a way to trigger his Shadow powers. The moment that happens, he'll tip the scales and one court will rule the world."

Didn't sound that bad to me. "Call me ignorant, but since you guys have been at war with each other for centuries, wouldn't that mean *peace*?"

"Yeah, but at what cost?" His gaze bore into mine and pictures began to flood my mind.

Limp bodies drained of blood; cut off heads with gaping mouths that revealed holes where there once used to be fangs; gaunt creatures clad in rags, with eyes as dead as a corpse's; and then lots of fire burning down everything in its wake.

I shook my head to get rid of the disturbing images. "I don't understand." My mouth felt dry, my tongue stuck to the back of my throat.

Aidan moistened his lips, hesitating. "Legend is, a famous Lore Court Seer once predicted the war between the Shadows, the vampires and the Lore court would escalate into the most brutal bloodbath the world has ever witnessed. This war will see many innocent victims. Two courts from three will perish. I don't know who will win, but I know it won't be the vampires, at least not us."

"And Layla wants to save the supernatural world?" I asked, not quite buying it. The woman loved blood and suffering. I couldn't see her as the savior she pretended to be.

"No, she's trying to save her ass," Aidan said. "Just as much as I'm trying to save ours. If it takes working with that vicious snake, then so be it."

In other words, we'd stuck with a power driven demi-goddess, who'd never warm up to the idea of me being Aidan's girlfriend. Sooner or later she'd try to get rid off me. "What's the plan?"

"I don't know." Aidan moistened his lips. I wrapped my arms around him, drawing him close, not really seeing the magnitude of what he was saying. I mean, it was just a legend, and legends are nothing but the figment of one's imagination. Okay, more often than not, there's a tiny grain of truth to them, but everyone knows that grain is completely blown out of proportion. So what if that guy, Seth, carried the ancestry of two courts? It didn't mean anything. He had no powers, and even if he did, he had no idea how to use them. Someone would have to teach him. He had no connection to the Shadows and Layla's mother had left the Lore court, so there would be no one to show him the ways of a deity.

Seriously, both Aidan and Layla were being paranoid, and I harbored no interest in letting their unfounded paranoia grab hold of me as well.

"Maybe the Seer was wrong. Just look at Nostradamus. The guy couldn't predict a thing if his life depended on it," I said. Aidan shook his head. I slapped his arm playfully. "Look, I don't get why you're so worried. The legend's been around for centuries, and chances are it won't happen any time soon, maybe never. For your peace of mind, I suggest consulting Kieran's new love interest."

"Patricia?" Aidan's brows shot up.

"She's a Seer, right?"

An amused glint appeared in his blue gaze. "Yeah, but she's also Cass's aunt *and* a fallen angel. That's not a trustworthy combination."

I shrugged. "I was just trying to give you an option. I'll help you find Seth, and then you'll see all those worry lines you got were for nothing." My finger trailed over his smooth forehead, lingering at this temple. His lips searched mine; his tongue explored my mouth as his hand wandered to my neck, sending shivers down my spine. We fell into a chair and I climbed on top of him, giving into his embrace, ready to help him forget his sorrows for a while. But as much as I knew we had nothing to worry about, a speck of doubt settled at the back of my mind, and no matter how hard I tried to push it away, I just couldn't stop thinking about it.

Chapter 10

It was late afternoon when Aidan announced he had to leave again, which suited me just fine. As much as I liked spending the day with him making out on the sofa, relationships don't usually work that way. One has to keep it mysterious, you know, be available for a time, and then pull back so the chase can start all over again. If Aidan wanted to hang out at the Lore Court without me, I wouldn't play the clingy girlfriend because it just wasn't my style. I was perfectly capable of entertaining myself in his absence. In fact so much that I planned to completely forget about him and really get into my new project, Paranormal Initiation. Finding Angel would be my first assignment.

I programmed Brendan's phone number into my cell and tossed the paper away. Then I slipped into my favorite pair of jeans and a tight shirt, pulled my hair up in a messy ponytail, and took my place at Aidan's shiny mahogany desk that smelled a tad too much of wood polish. Brendan needed my help or, better said, we both needed each other's help because I harbored no false hope of never seeking blood again. I sat there for a long time, recalling the few conversations I ever had with Angel and jotting everything down. By the time I finished, I thought I'd have a few scribbled pages and plenty of hints. And then I looked down and groaned inwardly because I had just wasted an hour on three bullet points.

First, Angel told me the Shadows took her in when she was just a little girl with no family and no hope of a future. Basically, she had spent seventeen years trapped in a mountain, watched by a bunch of creepy-eyed weirdos, like Kieran called them. As much as I would've wanted to disagree, they were kinda weird and I didn't fail to point that out when I first met Angel, probably helping her realize that her circumstances weren't exactly common among teens.

Second, she missed seeing the outside world, but she wasn't unhappy, or so she claimed. And, last but not least, right before Aidan freed me from Shadowland, I gave Angel the option to leave with me, but she wouldn't. Her exact words were that she'd die if she ever tried to escape. She never talked about Brendan, but she was curious about the bond I shared with Aidan, as though she was trying to find out more about it. I figured, at her age there's always a guy involved. She might've even been in love with him. Whether it was indeed Brendan, I couldn't tell.

I tapped my pen against my lips, putting two and two together. I doubted Angel was kidnapped because Shadowland was better fortified than Buckingham Palace or the White House. Thrain, Clare and Aidan's ex-BFF Blake managed to get in, but only because Thrain was a shape shifter and impersonated Devon so the guards would open the gates. Angel's disappearance had to be her own choice, meaning she knew what she was doing and she certainly knew how to get out of that place since she practically grew up there. However, if her fears of breaking out of the joint were founded, her actions could only mean one thing: sure death.

Had Angel become so desperate to get away that she decided to risk her life? The thought sat in the pit of my stomach like a rock. I swallowed hard, forcing myself to remain calm rather than let my emotions overwhelm me. Wanting to get away wasn't a strong enough motive. She could've easily left when I offered to help her escape. Something else must've triggered her sudden departure. Someone came after her with such a vengeance, making—maybe even *threatening*—her to leave, that Angel had no choice but to risk her life and leave her bonded mate behind. It was a far-fetched explanation based on nothing but my own reasoning. However, it was my only trail right now.

I was no Sherlock Holmes, but I was sure Scotland Yard would be proud of my brilliant detective skills and determination to seek out every clue and leave no stone unturned. I scribbled 'foul play' and 'possible suspect might be someone she trusted' on my notepad. In the event someone was hiding or even helping her, I also jotted down 'possible hiding places'. Then I pulled out a map of the Scottish Highlands and a compass to mark a thirty mile radius because that's how far I thought she'd get on foot before she had to stop, exhausted and hungry, maybe even doubting the sanity of her idea. I peered at the map with vast patches of green and brown indicating woods and mountains. Thirty square miles was a huge distance to cross but not impossible, and certainly not for a vampire who could move as fast as I could. Trouble was Aidan instructed me to stay within the safety of his fortress. Leaning against the chair, I considered my options: defy Aidan's wishes and leave the house, which might put both of us at risk because I knew if something happened to me he'd come running. Or call Brendan and share my meager findings with him, and let him take it from here.

With an exasperated sigh, I flicked my cell phone open and speed-dialed the first number saved as a shortcut.

"Brendan? It's Amber," I whispered even though I didn't need to lower my voice because there was no one around. For a moment, my heartbeat drowned out the silence on the other end of the line, and then someone's sharp tone made my heart skip a beat.

"How do you know Brendan?"

I flinched at Devon's voice. For a moment I considered faking a Chinese accent while claiming I had dialed the wrong number. Then I realized that might not work out so well after revealing my name. Damn, I had to stop doing that when I called people. But luckily for me, I had been friends with the whacky Cass long enough to adopt her ways of playing dumb, so my brain came up with a second plan. "Hey you." I smiled even though he couldn't see me. "What's up?"

"You tell me."

"How would I know when *you* called *me*?"

"How could I have when my phone rang?" Devon said, dryly.

That was Devon's number? Why would Brendan pretend to give me a number with the invitation to call him when it belonged to his blood brother or whatever sort of relatives they were? I tapped my fingers on the table, a bit irritated with both Devon for picking up and Brendan for giving me the wrong phone number in the first place. And then I realized I speed-dialed one instead of two; one was Devon's number, two belonged to Brendan. Due to my own stupidity I rang the wrong Shadow. "Right. Listen, I'd love to help but I'm kinda busy. Would you mind passing your phone over to Brendan?"

"He's not around." A pause on the other end of the line, then, "Where did you say you know him from?"

As far as I remembered I didn't, and that's exactly how I wanted it to stay. I was about to tell Devon to mind his own affairs—well, not in those words, think more along the lines of, *piss off, mate*—when I heard something across the room. I pushed the phone away from my ear and inclined my head as I strained to listen. There it was again, the softest scratching on wood coming from the window, slow and deliberate, reminding me of a rodent digging something up. And then it stopped.

"Amber? Are you still there?" Devon said. I couldn't deal with him right now. Not with a voice at the back of my mind, warning me to run as fast as I could. Running's always a good option, but first I had to find out what I was running from.

"Listen, I'd love to chat but I think I have a mouse problem," I whispered, my gaze still focused on the window.

"Mice?"

"Yeah, you know, they're furry animals with big eyes and long whiskers."

"Want me to call an exterminator?"

"What? And kill the little guy? I'd never hurt an animal...not even a spider!" Memories of me sucking a poor squirrel dry rushed through my mind. I shook my head. Basically, I was a huge hypocrite.

127

The scratching sound snapped me out of my thoughts.

"Gotta go," I whispered. Hanging up before Devon could resume his chatter, I tiptoed around the desk and toward the window. I knew I was being silly, and yet I couldn't control my racing heart, which I wasn't even sure was normal for a vampire.

I reached the window in a few short strides and peered out onto the beautiful backyard with its meticulously trimmed lawn and wilted rosebushes. Pressing a hand against my chest, I scanned the area. Nothing there. The sun was setting over the horizon in an array of colors, casting a soft, orange glow across the sky and over the hills. Smiling weakly at my own paranoia, I took a deep breath and turned away when the scratching began again, but this time it didn't stop.

I swear I could hear the pitter-patter of tiny feet scampering up and down the wall, gnawing and more clawing. Great. Now we had mice living inside the walls, which freaked me out big time. Maybe Aidan could buy some catch and release traps because, despite my past indiscretion and my phobia of anything with sharp teeth, I really didn't want to see an animal hurt or killed.

The clawing became more frantic. The temperature dropped a few degrees. It was so cold, my breath fogged up the glass. I wrapped my arms around my waist to keep from shivering as my supernatural senses went into full alert. Alarm sirens went off at the back of my head, warning me of something that was about to take place. But I had never been the brightest star at interpreting big, flashing neon lights, and particularly not the ones that indicate signs and omens.

Frozen to the spot, my gaze fell upon the wooden floor right under my feet and the three fifteen inch scratches embedded deep into the cherry wood that I swear weren't there half an hour ago. It had to be some sort of prank, one part of my mind argued, just like the incident with the different eye colors at Cass's birthday party. But who would play a prank on me? There was no one around to do it...unless they were invisible. Like a—

Ghost.

Chapter 11

My eyes widened when the word registered in my brain. I groaned. Please, not again. I was a medium bestowed with the ability to see and talk with dead people, but, like Aidan liked to put it, I was a chicken scared of my own shadow. My poor brain quickly retrieved all the information on ghosts I had gathered in my eighteen years of life.

They were creepy and scared the hell out of any normal person, and some did it for no apparent reason, think a typical poltergeist haunting.

More often than not, they were confused and needed assistance in order to leave the physical plane.

And some couldn't rest unless they concluded their business, which was left unfinished upon their unexpected departure from our world.

I could only hope my ghost fell into category number two, because anything else would have me packing my bags in no time. When all that blood started pouring down the walls and dripping inside Brendan's mouth, I thought I was just hallucinating from hunger. I mean, you don't usually see walls or people drenched in blood unless it's in the movies, but this wasn't Hollywood, so it couldn't be remotely true. The scratches, however, sounded like a sure-thing spirit haunting sign if I had ever heard of one. I was having an *Exorcist* moment, and that freaked me out big time. Spiritual love bond or not, I wouldn't be living under the same roof with a creepy ghost. Aidan had two options, either call in an exorcist to banish this thing forever, or we'd move, and preferably a long distance away from here.

An icy breeze blew across my cheeks. In spite of the cold, sweat poured down my back, soaking my clothes. Swallowing hard, I staggered back away from the eerie scratches and the window and turned to make a quick dash out the door when it slammed shut in my face. I was pretty sure it wasn't the wind, especially when the knob started to turn.

"Who's there?" I shouted. No one answered. The door started to shake in its hinges. A few droplets of blood roll down the wood ever so slowly, as though to mock me. Okay, I wasn't going to stick around for Act Two of 'Bloody Walls'. I had to get the heck out of here by any means possible.

I had two options: either jump out the window or dash through the haunted, blood-spattered door, which was only a few feet away but might not open.

The ground below the window might just take a bit longer to reach, but it sure was the more inviting option. Only, I wasn't keen on finding out whether my vampire body could take the fall without a sprained ankle. Okay, I was being a drama queen because Aidan's workplace was situated on the second floor and I had yet to hear of anyone dying from this height, but inflicting any sort of pain on myself deliberately wasn't my thing.

Damn Aidan for not briefing me in if my new body could jump out a window without hurting myself. Or whether being immortal also included the perks of not feeling any pain.

The squeal of sharp nails dragging along wood made me jump. Glancing across the room, I could see more scratch marks appearing before my eyes, as though something were pulling itself toward me, grinding its claws into the boards as it inched closer. I dug my nails into the soft flesh of my arms and weighed the pros and cons of jumping vs. door.

Ah, toss it. There was no way I was going to hover around and have a confrontation with this undead thing. I dashed for the door and turned the knob, but it wouldn't open. I pulled and kicked at it with every bit of my immortal strength I possessed, and still, it wouldn't budge an inch. Crap! The only option left was...

Opening the window, I climbed on the windowsill and pinching my nose—no idea why I did that—I jumped into the depth of the backyard, landing ungracefully on my butt with a loud *thud*. It didn't hurt, which I attributed to my genes and their tendency to store fat in all the wrong places. Thanks, Mom, for that.

I got up and brushed my clothes, peering up at the open window. The stiff, wine-colored brocade curtains barely moved in the strong breeze preceding the usual Scottish rainfall, but somehow I could sense something up there. A faceless entity, if you will. I was a necromancer, for crying out loud. Why couldn't I see it? Maybe my ability was latent. Or maybe it was just the negative residue of a long-lost ghost that had already passed into the light or gone straight to Hell.

Who was I kidding? I obviously had a full-blown poltergeist haunting on my hands. Call it intuition, but I had the strange feeling I'd be jumping out of more windows in the near future.

From the corner of my eye, I thought I caught movement behind the curtain. Holding my breath, I stared up at the empty space and listened for any sound. Seconds ticked by. And then the curtain moved again. My heart skipped a beat. I wanted to run but my legs were frozen to the spot; my eyes were compelled to watch.

Wisps of inky mist swirled in front of the window a moment before invisible hands closed it...ever so slowly, and then slammed it shut, making me jump. I pinched myself. Hard. Yeah, I was definitely awake. The window fogged over and a sketch appeared. I squinted to recognize the words: GET OUT!

Basically, the ghost was kicking me out. I felt faint, even though my heart was beating a million miles an hour. My hands were ice cold, and my legs threatened to give way under me. Forcing my gaze away from the window, I retrieved my phone from my pocket and, with shaking hands, speed-dialed Aidan's number. The line rang twice before going to voicemail, so I left an urgent message to get back to the house and that it was a matter of life and death. I barely got to flick my phone shut when the air sizzled and he appeared, looking gloomy yet very yummy in his jeans and unbuttoned black leather coat.

"Aidan?" I asked, inching away from him, because I couldn't be sure it was he indeed. In my panic, I thought the ghost might be playing a trick on me so I'd fall into a trap.

"What's wrong?" His brows were furrowed, fear mirrored in his expression. And then I noticed what looked like a burning whip in his hand. I had seen that thing before.

"Is that—" My throat constricted at the memory of a stranger chasing me in the woods, holding the exact same thing in his hand. I remembered the whip cutting through the air like a knife, hitting a tree only a few inches away from me, and leaving a burning trail in its wake. It could've killed me, yet for weeks Aidan claimed it was nothing and refused to show me what it really looked like.

"Why are you outside? Anything happen?" Aidan hurried to hide the whip inside his coat and grabbed me in a tight embrace.

I peered into his blue gaze filled with worry, wondering whether I should make a scene because of the whip and the fact that he obviously still had no intention to open up about his bounty hunter past, or make a scene because of the ghost. I figured the apparition was the greater urgency. I'd get to the whip later.

"There's a ghost inside. I had to jump out the window. Look at my favorite jeans. They're ruined." I paused for effect as I showed him the big brown mud stain on my backside. Focusing on the jeans helped me avoid a full-blown panic attack. Aidan peered from my butt to the closed windows and raised a brow but didn't comment. I pointed up. "You don't believe me. Just look at the writing."

"What writing?"

I glanced up. The letters had vanished together with any sign of my poltergeist. "The house's haunted, Aidan." I sounded whiny but I couldn't help myself. "I'm not going back in there. That's a category number one ghost. And I was really hoping it was going to be a category two." From his puzzled expression I figured he didn't understand a word. "We have a poltergeist on our hands."

"Amber—" He hesitated. I held my hand up to stop him.

"Trust me, I know what I'm talking about. This wasn't a happy little spirit passing through. What I just experienced was dark and evil. And I have proof. Upstairs." He drew a long breath as I continued, "Claw marks embedded into your precious floor. And not just any claw marks, but huge ones. When you see them, you're going to swear Wolverine from X-men was here. They're at least fifteen inches long."

He crossed his arms over his chest, regarding me. The worry lines were still there. "Let's go take a look, shall we? Tell me what happened on the way up." I didn't want to but I had to show him the house was haunted, so I let him grab my hand, dragging me after him, as I recounted every tiny detail. We reached the second floor. Aidan entered first, I followed a step behind.

"It's freezing in here," he said. "Did you turn on the air conditioner full blast?"

"It was the ghost." I sucked in a deep breath as I peered around me, from the door to the window. There was no blood in sight. The claw marks had disappeared completely.

I ran over to the window and knelt down, then swiped my fingers across the smooth wood, whispering, "It was right here. I swear it was."

"You're safe now," Aidan said. He scooped me up in his arms. I buried my head against his chest, wondering what the heck was going on? Was I losing my mind?

"Out of curiosity, you said you jumped out a window. Why didn't you use the door?"

"I couldn't. The ghost wouldn't let me," I said. "I'm telling you, it's evil." His expression told me he wasn't convinced. "You believe me, don't you?"

Aidan tensed, hesitating. "Amber, this world's new to you. Obviously, you're having trouble adapting to your necromancer abilities. Give it a few more weeks, and you'll see everything will click into place. This gift wasn't meant to be a curse but a blessing. Many immortals would kill for it."

"Lucky me. Can't you have Layla remove it...you know, since you guys are such close buddies now?"

He shook his head. "We've been through this over and over again. I wish I could find someone to get rid of it, but only Layla can take it back, and she won't do it." I could see I was losing his attention by the way his eyes darted across the room, like his mind was already thinking of a million other things he could be doing instead of listening to my drivel.

"Then you need to do something about this poltergeist, otherwise I'm not staying here."

"You're always imaging the worst case scenario," he said. "I'm sure it's just a lost, harmless ghost bored out of his mind. Maybe it's trying to get your attention." I opened my mouth to speak when he cut me off. "Don't get me wrong, I'm glad you're safe, but I don't think you have anything to worry about. If an evil ghost resided here, Cass would've told us the last time she visited. Besides, the house is secured by magic so it's impossible for anything powerful to enter. Maybe it was just an animal spirit." The concern in his eyes disappeared and an amused glint took its place. "I think you jumped out the window for nothing."

For a second relief washed over me. That the spirit could be an animal didn't cross my mind, but it made sense...for all of three seconds or as long as it took me to realize animals can't spell.

"How do you explain the window closing right after I jumped?"

"You know the backdoor's always open. The sudden draft might've slammed the window shut. So, laws of physics?" he suggested.

I nodded, even though I knew better. It was a poltergeist.

"You're so lucky I beat you in that paranormal race, Aidan. Otherwise, ghosts would be bugging the crap out of you."

"They're just passing by and need a little guidance." He shrugged. "No big deal."

I smiled sweetly, unable to stop feeling resentful that my boyfriend wouldn't believe me. "You've helped me so much. I don't know what I'd do without you."

"I've been a shitty boyfriend in that I haven't spent much time with you lately, but I swear I'll make it up to you. Just give me a few more days to get this Lore court business sorted out, and then we can go somewhere nice, just the two of us. What do you think?" His strong arms pulled me close until his breath caressed my cheek.

"I'd love that," I whispered.

"Great." He placed a sloppy kiss on my lips and pulled back. The same absentminded expression from before appeared again. "See you tonight, then?"

I nodded, but he was already gone, leaving only the slightest hint of his cologne behind. I stared at the empty space for a while, wondering how he could be so blind and not notice that something weird was going on. The word 'blind' didn't even do him justice. More like completely and utterly clueless to anything that didn't have a big fat flashing neon light with the inscription 'weird things happening'.

Heaving a big sigh, I walked into the hallway and stopped to listen for any sounds from that poltergeist entity. But I knew it'd leave me alone...for the time being.

Chapter 12

After my encounter with the spirit and Aidan's departure, I didn't return to resume my work in his office. For one, I figured the ghost might still hover around. And then there was also the residue of the haunting that might trigger my abilities as a necromancer. I didn't fear for Aidan or Kieran's safety. They had never reported anything weird or freaky going on. Besides, I knew this thing had its sights on me. Even though I didn't want to be in the VIP section of this ghost's freak show, it seemed to save its performances only for me and I had no idea why.

In spite of Aidan's adamant reassurances that the house couldn't possibly be haunted, I knew better so I spent the whole afternoon trying to figure out what to do about my uninvited and invisible guest. Obviously, the only way to ascertain its intentions was to actually ask the entity upfront, but that wasn't even an option, what with me possibly fainting and all. I figured I could be more creative than that.

Being a huge fan of lists, I grabbed a piece of paper and pen, and made notes as I recalled what happened in order to figure out what could possibly have triggered the poltergeist activity. I had been analyzing Angel's disappearance. Maybe the ghost feared beings of light and turned all psycho when it mistook my friend's name for an actual angel. The explanation sounded a bit farfetched, but I didn't disregard it.

What else did I have? The woods. The forest outside the mansion was mysterious and held onto countless secrets. A few days after my arrival in Scotland, my friend, Clare, told me the townspeople in Inverness were scared of the woods because people had disappeared in the past. Was it foul play, like murder? Had their lonely spirits wandered into the house, seeking my help? Possible but not likely since, as far as I knew, and I agree I didn't know much, entities were usually bound to a place such as a house or the woods, but they couldn't travel to and fro.

Then there was the phone call during which I first heard the scratching sound coming from the window. I could feel a deeper meaning here, as though my sixth sense was telling me something, but no matter how hard my mind tried to put the puzzle pieces together, a connection wasn't clear. Could Devon have anything to do with the haunting? Highly doubtful because the Shadows were shaman warriors who, according to Aidan, wielded no power over the Otherworld. But why would a ghost have such a strong reaction to a conversation? It didn't make any sense unless...

I took a deep breath as I tapped my pen against my lips.

Maybe it wasn't so much the conversation as the person on the other end of the line? But why would Devon's voice trigger such a response from the ghost?

I made a few question marks next to the letter D and then put the pen aside, ready to move on to the next part of my plan: searching the house for any signs of someone dying in the past.

Careful not to touch anything, I combed the mansion meticulously, moving from room to room, leaving the one that was always locked last. The chamber once belonged to Aidan's ex, Rebecca. Rebecca was the one who turned him and bit me during my astral travel to the Otherworld. She fed on my soul's power, which in effect translated into major blood loss from my physical body. It all sounded so complicated, and yet it couldn't be more simple. At the time of my attack, she was dead, I wasn't. My soul was still connected to my body, so by drinking my soul's power, she inevitably took my blood, which strengthened her. And now she was looking for a way out of Hell's only dimension reserved for paranormal beings, Distros. Already she had fed on a reaper's blood, which allowed her to travel through the different dimensions of Hell. As much as Aidan wanted to believe Rebecca was gone forever, I knew it was only a matter of time until she twisted her way back into our lives.

A shiver ran down my spine as I rattled the door. My blood chilled, as though a dagger were being drawn up and down my spine, settling at the nape of my neck. It was wrong of me to defy Aidan's wishes that the door be kept locked at all times, but I couldn't help myself.

I still remembered the moment our eyes connected in the Otherworld. Her green gaze had been full of eternal hunger; her reddish brown hair had been caked to her scrawny shoulders where mud had dried to form dark patches. There had been something in her manner—preeminence, as though she had been born to rule and those around her were fated to obey her every command. Maybe it was a vampire thing to instill a sense of inferiority in others because I had felt the same way upon meeting Aidan.

Even though entering the room might activate my necromancer abilities, I needed to see her deathbed one more time because an inner voice told me I was missing something and I was ready to find out what that something was. The lock snapped open at my second pull. As I walked past, the door groaned in its hinges, as though to utter a silent warning. It was superstitious of me to believe such nonsense, yet, I took it as a sign to hurry.

The room looked just the way I remembered it: high ceiling, paneled walls, and a shiny wooden floor.

To my right was a four-poster bed carved with half-moons and beautiful roses as large as my palm; to my left was a huge wardrobe, which had been once filled to the brim with marvelous silk and brocade dresses in all possible colors. Only now, after being bitten by her, could I understand Aidan's hesitation to discard her belongings. Like him, I felt her terrible magic pulling me to her, drawing me into her world of beauty, lies, and deceit. And if the spell of her bite was so strong on me, then I didn't even want to imagine its effect on Aidan who had been Rebecca's slave for many years before breaking her terrible bond by killing her.

I gingerly opened the door to her wardrobe and peered at the vacant space, wondering what happened to her clothes. Did Aidan clear out her stuff? And if so, why did he do it? Something began to throb inside me. It took me a while to realize it was disbelief. I knew I should be happy. Knowing Aidan, he probably donated all of her clothes to charity, and yet, for some inexplicable reason, I wasn't thrilled. I felt as though it wasn't right and he had done her injustice. A spark of anger pulsed inside me, as though in agreement. Aidan was the most reasonable person I had ever met. He never initiated a step without considering possible consequences. That he threw away her belongings after keeping them for centuries had to mean something, but I couldn't see the logic.

Why couldn't I understand his motives? He was with me now; he didn't want her back. Maybe

Rebecca's spell on me was stronger than I initially imagined because my feelings made no sense whatsoever.

I closed the door to Rebecca's former chamber and returned to my room to wait for Aidan.

* * *

"You disposed of her belongings," I whispered as soon as Aidan stepped into my moonlit bedroom. He didn't reply as he slipped out of his leather coat and tossed it over the back of a chair, then sat down on the bed, keeping a few inches between us. He kept his gaze averted from me, but I could sense he knew exactly what I was talking about.

"It was time to leave that part of my life behind me," Aidan said, sitting down on the edge of the bed. "Make a new beginning. With you."

I inched closer and took a whiff of the unfamiliar smell on him. The tiniest hint of lavender and roses, of green valleys and ripe red grapes hit my nostrils. I took a deep breath and let the pleasant aroma wash over me, making me feel all sorts of emotions I had been trying to push to the back of my mind ever since meeting Aidan.

A strong sense of longing grabbed hold of me. I had to touch him. I had to have him this instant, wrap my thighs around him and let him introduce me to what he had been eager to show me for weeks.

He looked so handsome with his dark tousled hair and his shirt unbuttoned to reveal just a little bit of his taunt skin and burly chest. I moistened my lips and reached out to trail my fingers down his neck, stopping at the button of his shirt. With a flick of my fingers, I unfastened the first, then went on to loosen the rest of them, and slipped my hands inside his shirt to push it aside.

Aidan's breath caught in his throat. I moved a few inches back to marvel at his sculpted chest, gaping in delight at his strong muscles and soft skin. I could feel his heartbeat quickening beneath my exploring fingers. My chin jutted up just an inch, proud of how I could make him shiver by just running my fingers up and down his torso.

"Amber." His voice sounded hoarse, barely louder than a whisper.

Smiling, I increased the pressure as I dug my nails into his skin and watched the soft red lines forming. His tongue flicked over his lower lip, leaving a wet trail behind as his gaze bore into mine, prodding, questioning. Something pulsed within me, making me want to explore every inch of his skin. Determined to have him there and then, I rose on my knees to press my mouth against his, and spread my lips just a tiny bit to welcome his tongue. His palms wandered beneath my shirt as he pulled me onto his lap. I settled against him and wrapped my legs around his waist, my hands already fighting with his jeans.

"No." He pulled back and turned away from me.

I stared at him in disbelief. Did he just brush me off? "What's wrong?"

He shook his head, avoiding my gaze. "You're not really ready for this, Amber."

"Isn't that up to me to decide? I can assure you I feel more than ready. In fact, I want it. Now." And boy was that true. My whole body was on fire, begging for his touch. I had never felt so much desire for anyone before. It was a sign. Aidan and I were meant to be together, so why not take our relationship to the next level?

"No, babe, you don't understand." He turned around and grabbed my hand only to drop it an instant later, as though he had just been burned. "This isn't you. It's succubus energy lingering on me that's making you want to jump into bed with me. I don't expect you to understand now. You will after I've taken a shower and washed this stench off of me. Wait here. I'll be right back."

My gaze remained glued to the door long after he closed it behind him as his words' meaning slowly sank in. The strong longing began to dissipate, but it didn't leave me completely.

When he returned a few minutes later, I had gathered my composure and straightened my disheveled clothes. Or so I thought. His hair and skin, glistening with moisture, made my heart skip a beat again. He was wrong. It wasn't just succubus energy. My feelings were the real deal and I couldn't get enough of him.

"Are you okay?" Aidan asked softly as he returned to his previous position at the far end of my bed. "You're back to your old self again?"

I shrugged. Trust the guy to know how to make a girl feel special after she almost jumped his bones. "You make it sound like a bit of passion's such a bad thing."

"Not this kind, Amber. It's not *natural*." He took a deep breath, his gaze darkening. "I dread the moment I enter the Lore court and count the seconds until I can leave again. There's nothing normal about wanting someone so bad you'd literally kill for that instant gratification."

"So, when you're there you feel that way about *everyone*?" I made it sound nonchalant, as though I didn't care, but inside, my temper boiled over, waiting to find a way out like an erupting volcano.

"Pretty much." Aidan nodded. "But they're succubi. It's their nature to make you feel that way."

He meant, all horny and eager to peel off their clothes. I snorted. The guy was digging himself a big hole here. The last few weeks, Aidan had tried to get inside my knickers at every available opportunity. I thought that consuming passion he couldn't control was something special, you know, the result of our bond. Now I was slowly starting to think he had just been pushy like every other guy out there who couldn't keep it in his pants.

"Is that why you're not taking me to the Lore court? Because you think I couldn't take the sexual heat?"

He laughed briefly and started drawing circles in my palm. "What you just experienced was barely a fragment of what you can expect in there. I don't want to lose you. There's nothing wrong with wanting to protect the ones you love." I rolled my eyes inwardly and opened my mouth to protest when Aidan cut me off. I sensed a deliberate change of subject. "So, what've you been up to? Any progress with your new project?" He leaned back against my cover and propped his arms behind his back, signaling the conversation was over.

"Are you hiding something?" I asked.

"What makes you say that?" His surprise looked fake, planted on his beautiful face to fool me into thinking I had it all wrong. I wasn't going to drop the topic.

"You let the succubi touch you?"

"It's not a matter of choice, Amber. They just do that when they walk past or when you don't move out of their way fast enough." His superior tone enraged me.

"I want to come with you. I need to see what's going on in there since I'm a part of that world now."

He shook his head vehemently. Something sparkled in his blue gaze. "No. That's out of the question."

149

A stray vision rolled before my eyes, making me stop my unspoken protest.

A shed in the woods, surrounded by tall trees that filtered the sunlight. A squeaking door hanging off its hinges. Angel's jet-black hair, now covered in mud and dry leaves; her eyes filled with fear and unshed tears; her lips quivering, as though she daren't speak...or scream. And then I felt someone else's presence. Someone was guarding her, watching her every step.

That Aidan was dealing with succubi was bad enough, that he hid something else from me was far worse. I made a mental note to find out his secret, but now wasn't the time. I had more pressing matters.

"I need to speak to you about Angel," I said slowly. Aidan barely looked up from the sheath he untied from his ankle.

"Can it wait, babe? I've been busy all day, I just want to close my eyes and go to sleep."

A nap? That was his 'polite' excuse for not wanting to talk. Yeah, I was learning to read him quite well. You've been avoiding me for days, I wanted to yell at him. But being needy wasn't my style. Besides, Cosmo always said a girl's got to shape a guy into fitting into the relationship just like you make room for a new wallet in your handbag, not the other way around. I was going at it the wrong way.

I grabbed his hand, forcing him to look at me. "I think something weird is happening. I can feel it."

"I'm pretty sure everything's fine." His expression remained cool and composed. If it weren't for the tiny shadow clouding his eyes for a second, I'd never have thought he was lying.

"The house is haunted, Aidan. I saw huge scratches on the floor. The window shut in my face."

"I thought we decided it was just an animal spirit."

"It wasn't an animal!" My eyes threw daggers, warning him to tread carefully.

"I believe you," Aidan said. His gaze implored me to trust him. "You know I'd never doubt a word you say. I just wish I could've had a look at them."

"Well, next time I'll make sure to snap a picture on my cell phone while I'm running for my life. Maybe I'll throw in some factual comments, like in a documentary." I moistened my lips as I considered my words. "Look, there's more. I can feel someone's presence." My gaze bore into him, prodding his mind, which remained surprisingly blank.

"That's part of the gift."

"No. This isn't your average soul in need." I lowered my voice. "Something sinister, *unnatural*, is watching me. I'm telling you, it's pure evil."

His fingers stroked my hand. "We talked about this, Amber. It's your gift kicking into first gear. I'm really trying to figure out how to keep the spirits at bay, but you need to give me more time. Trust me, you have nothing to fear." His gorgeous lips curved into his usual breathtaking smile. It was a blatant lie. My heart filled with love but also something else. Fear. Dread. A premonition I couldn't quite pinpoint.

151

Aidan knew something was happening. And yet he chose not to share it with me. I should've told him about Brendan and Angel but I couldn't. The Shadows were his enemies and he had been looking for a way to defeat them for centuries. Aidan would do anything to destroy them, especially after they tricked me into striking a deal with them behind Aidan's back so I'd help them find the Book of the Dead Rebecca stole many centuries ago. My deal with them had been a bad move, which led to my physical death. However, Aidan didn't understand that not every Shadow was to blame. Angel was innocent.

I sat up and returned the smile, deliberately hiding my thoughts from him in case he focused on them. My mind began to unravel the puzzle. Aidan being all mysterious and secretive. The sudden disappearance of a friend around the time a ghost began to haunt me. Paranormal activity when Aidan wasn't around. Seriously, what were the odds of no connection? I had been living in Aidan's mansion for weeks and nothing particular happened until three days ago. Something or someone triggered the ghost activity, maybe even brought the entity into this house by accident.

Who knew what Aidan was up to at the enigmatic Lore Court? I had a strong feeling that secretive place was responsible for this haunting and wished I could see the place for myself. Curiosity consumed me. Two things registered at the back of my mind: It was time to find out, both what happened to Angel and what the Lore court was like.

But before I did, I had to find a way to increase my strength. Drinking blood wasn't an option—it might just be a necessity in case I had to fight to rescue Angel and teleport our way out of there rather than walk.

Chapter 13

A rush of nail-biting anxiety flooded over me as I planned out my covert mission into the mysterious woods. I had to make sure nobody saw me. Naturally, official jungle green camouflage would be my first choice, but how fashionable was that? Besides, where would I find a shop selling that in the middle of nowhere? So I settled for black, not least because it made me look slimmer.

Dawn was hours away when I rolled out of bed and rummaged through my wardrobe in search of a pair of jeans and a black shirt that wouldn't reflect the moonlight. The house was quiet as a tomb. Aidan had long left with the promise of being back soon. For once, I hoped he wouldn't keep true to his word because what I was about to do might just take longer than anticipated. Particularly with my crappy sense of direction—or lack thereof.

The moon cast a silver glow on the backyard. Apart from the rustling of leaves, my heightened senses picked up no movement. Out of habit, I blew a hot breath into my cold hands and mentally prepared for the sprint ahead of me. Of course I could try to teleport but I knew I'd just be wasting my strength. My body felt too weak, in major need for blood. So I had to settle for running.

My boots made no sound as my legs moved swiftly, minding the dry twigs and branches that might give away my presence to those invisible eyes constantly watching Aidan's property. I cut through the garden and jumped over the fence in one swift movement. As I reached the woods, the house disappeared in the distance, swallowed by the impenetrable pitch black around me. The dense canopy of trees filtered the weak rays of moonlight, but I didn't need to rely on any source of light to know the direction I had to take.

About an hour from Aidan's property there was a shed, hidden In the Scottish Highlands. I had been there before. In fact, one could say entering that little shed was the beginning of all my sorrows and doom. If it weren't for my brother's stupid plan to steal a bag of worthless jewels, I might've never entered Layla's paranormal race and scooped up the first prize that granted me the ability to talk with the dead for the next five hundred years, or until Aidan's enemies managed to cut off my head because I was a vampire now—whichever came first. Yeah, that's what family does to you. I couldn't even disown Dallas since, in the mortal world, I was basically dead and had no dime to my name.

Under normal circumstances, my mortal brain combined with my lack of any sense of direction would've gotten me lost in no time. But being a vampire came with a few perks. I remembered the way to the shed as if the trek with my brother happened only yesterday. With the help of my unnatural speed, I sprinted down the valley and then up the hills again, dashing through the thicket as I let my legs carry me, barely breaking a sweat. I reached the narrow path winding up to the shed and stopped, leaning against a tree as I scanned the area, watching my surroundings for any sign that I wasn't alone.

During that fateful night when I stole the jewels, the hut had been deserted. But only because Aidan had tied the other paranormal beings to a tree so he could solve the riddle and pick up the right jewels in Layla's race. I harbored no false hope that my crappy luck would be on my side and no one would be here to hinder me. Minding my movements, I crouched and inched through the bushes as fast as I could, all the while straining my ears to listen for any unusual sound.

I circled the shed twice but saw no sign of life. If anyone was around, they either had left on their coffee break, or they knew how to blend in with the night so not even my vampire vision could spot them. I figured I had two options: keep wasting time by waiting until someone popped out of the shadows, or hope for the best and walk in in the hope whoever guarded this shed didn't take their duties too seriously.

Ah, toss it.

Patience had never been one of my virtues. Besides, I didn't have *forever*. Aidan might return to the mansion any minute and notice my disappearance. I couldn't risk him finding out I had broken my promise to stay inside. I jumped up from my crouching position and reached the door in two long strides, my boots barely making any sound on the naked ground, then stopped to look around me one last time.

The moon hid behind a curtain of thick clouds. The trees cast ominous shadows across the soft grass and fallen leaves. Apart from the strong breeze blowing through the thicket, I heard nothing.

Time to walk in then.

Taking a deep breath, I yanked the door open a few inches, cringing at the squeaky sound of old hinges, and squeezed inside the shed. In my previous life, I once needed a flashlight to find my way around, but now my eyes only took a few seconds to adjust to the pitch black.

The room looked much larger than I remembered with whitewashed walls and a wooden floor covered in dust. To the far right was a chair, to my left a window. Last time I was here, there had been a hole in the floor under the window, filled with worthless gemstones concealed by a huge layer of mud. The altar with the scroll that contained the Riddle for Sight was gone now, but in its place I found something else.

My stomach churning, I knelt down and pressed my nose against the floor to smell the familiar scent. Dust particles tickled the back of my throat as I inhaled deeply, gorging on the aroma that should've been forbidden to me but proved so irresistible.

Blood.

Just a few drops but enough to tell me someone had been hurt. Maybe Angel had put up a good fight and managed to escape her aggressor. Now I was getting carried away. There was no sign of a fight, not even of anyone's recent visit. I rubbed my hand against the dried drops of blood and licked it clean. It still tasted fresh, then again I wasn't exactly a connoisseur in that department. My stomach rumbled and a soft tremor rocked my body, demanding more of the delicious stuff.

I wiped my hand over my jeans and inspected the naked floor and walls for a trapdoor or hidden entrance. Nothing. My frustration grew as I swept over my surroundings once again without much success. I knew this was the right shed because this place had been the stuff of my biggest nightmares. I'd recognize it in a heartbeat, and yet I had to be wrong because it seemed too quiet, too undisturbed. Ready to give up, I reached the door when the moon broke behind the clouds and a soft light fell through the window. The glowing ray fell on something on the floor—a tiny object that had also been in my nightmares for weeks.

With shaky fingers I grabbed the shard of a mirror, as large as my palm, and held it up to inspect it closer, my heart beating frantically against my chest. It was just a mirror. Any mirror. Not the same as the one that caught my attention from under a bush prior to Rebecca's attack in the Otherworld. Seriously, stumbling upon a mirror under a bush in the middle of nowhere might be odd but could still be attributed to coincidence. Finding one again just a few weeks later, and this time in a deserted shed—now, what were the odds?

Ever since my attack, I hated mirrors, and I couldn't help myself. My body shuddered. My legs threatened to buckle under me. Tiny rivulets of sweat ran down my spine, and my breathing came in ragged heaps. If I didn't know any better, I might just be inclined to think I was having my first panic attack as a vampire. Or second, considering what I went through with that poltergeist less than twenty-four hours ago.

"Come on, you idiot. Get a grip," I whispered to myself. But it didn't help.

I closed my eyes and slowly counted to ten, then opened them again, forcing myself to look at the thing because I wasn't going to develop a phobia of mirrors—if that was even a valid clinical condition. I rotated the tiny object in my hand to inspect it closer.

The surface was clean and smooth; two of its edges were uneven, as though it had been chipped off a larger piece. It was too dark to see much else, so I pushed it inside my back pocket and headed out the door, making sure to close it behind me, when I felt someone's presence a moment before a hand covered my mouth.

Chapter 14

"Why am I not surprised to see you?" Aidan hissed in my ear. His hot breath caressed my skin, making me shiver with pleasure even though I wasn't exactly pleased to see him.

"I could ask you the same thing," I hissed back against his palm. He dropped his hand from my mouth and spun me around to face him. We were surrounded by darkness, but I could make out his shimmering eyes, pale skin and strong cheekbones. His hair—a tad too long now—brushed his cheeks and spilled over the collar of his leather coat. He looked so badass I could've tossed him against the nearest tree and snogged his face off. Then I realized it might be the succubus energy residue on him making me have lots of naughty thoughts.

"I see you met your friends again." I clicked my tongue and shot him a reproachful look.

"Huh?" He shook his head, irritated. "Amber, what are you doing here?"

I shrugged. "Going for a walk?"

"You could've done that in our backyard. And please keep your voice down. We wouldn't want to wake up London." He grabbed my arm. I expected him to squeeze but his hand just lingered there, almost caressing my skin. "Seriously, what are you doing here? Robbing the neighborhood like last time?" He pointed at my black ensemble.

"I was, uh, stargazing."

He laughed. "That excuse didn't fly last time and it won't now. So, what's with this outfit?"

"I knew I should have gone with the jungle camouflage," I mumbled.

"Apparently, black's in for crooks this autumn. You should've gotten the ski mask and gun to match." He smiled; his tone betrayed he was being sarcastic again.

I pushed him away and started down the narrow path in the direction I had come from as I mumbled, "If you *must* know, I was getting a late night snack. Those fast food cravings are killing me." He snorted so I rolled my eyes. "Honestly, Aidan, if you're trying to be a comedian, don't give up your day job. Now, care to elaborate why *you* followed me?"

His hand clasped my waist, forcing me to stop in mid-stride. I turned slowly, my eyes throwing daggers. He might look irresistibly cute, but I didn't appreciate his stalking. I opened my mouth to give him a piece of my mind when his laughter stopped me.

"You think I'm stalking you?" He laughed again.

"Why's that funny? Am I not stalk-worthy?"

"I didn't say that." His gaze scanned the impenetrable shadows around us.

I elbowed him in the ribs. "Relax. I was just messing with you."

"I wasn't following you. I didn't even expect to find you here."

"But you were following *something* or *someone*." I regarded him intently, waiting for a sign that would betray his intentions. His expression remained unreadable.

"Can't tell you. It's part of the job," Aidan said.

Layla's job. The woman who wanted him so badly she almost killed me. I couldn't understand why he trusted her. Or why he'd even want to take that job. It didn't make sense. There was something in it for him. I just had to figure out what it was.

"Did you have a nice walk?" Aidan asked. The sarcasm in his voice didn't fail to register with me. I nodded enthusiastically.

"Definitely. I've come to realize I should go for a walk more often. The stars are just gorgeous this time of night."

His muscles tensed, but he didn't argue. "Let's get you home."

"What about your job?"

He hesitated for a moment before he replied. "I'll come back later." Meaning, he'd come back later when I wasn't around. I pushed my hand inside my pocket to touch the mirror. A tiny jolt of electricity surged through my fingers, making me flinch.

"You okay?" Aidan whispered.

"Yeah, just a bit cold."

"Here." He shrugged out of his coat and wrapped it around my shoulders.

"Thanks," I said, inhaling deeply. His scent made me shiver just like the electric jolt had, but it was with pleasure.

"Ready to go?"

Did I have a choice? I nodded and let him lead the way, wondering why we didn't just teleport. He sprinted through the trees with me following a few inches behind. A few times he turned to make sure I hadn't slowed down, and our eyes connected in that silent agreement that was part of our fated bond. Moving in the darkness, I felt the connection to him stronger than ever before, like a tiny thread that bound us together and drew us to one another no matter whether we were a few inches or hundreds of miles apart. The mere thought of being separated from him hurt me to the core.

We reached the hill overlooking the mansion when Aidan stopped and I almost bumped into him, lost in thought.

"What's wrong?" I whispered, almost expecting someone to jump out of the bushes and attack us.

Aidan wrapped his arms around me and pulled me close whispering in my ear, "I've missed you. I've been wanting to spend time with you for ages, even if it's just going for a jog through the woods."

"So that's why we didn't teleport." I smiled as his lips brushed my neck. His tongue began to trace slow circles beneath my earlobe, sending shivers of pleasure down my spine. His touch felt so good, I sighed softly and threw my head back to signal I wanted more. Aidan's hand reached beneath my top as he pressed me gently against a tree trunk and his mouth found mine in a hungry kiss.

In the darkness, I gave way into his embrace, letting his hand explore my skin beneath my clothes. His heart hammered against mine, harder and faster the more heated our kiss became. Slowly, a delicious fog enveloped my mind, making forming any sort of coherent thought impossible. I ran my fingers through his hair to pull him closer, and for a moment I actually hoped he'd take it as an invitation to do whatever he wanted.

"That's not what I had in mind," he whispered against my lips a second before he pulled back. I opened my eyes, ready to protest, already missing his touch on my skin.

"What did you have in mind then?" My voice came as hoarse as his, filled with yearning and disappointment. He had been trying to get me to sleep with him for ages, and now that he had the chance he wasn't taking it. The guy's reasoning made no sense whatsoever.

"I just wanted a bit of intimacy. That's all."

I nodded, not believing a word. No guy wanted to just cuddle. It was against their nature. My mind reached into his to search for an answer. It took me a while to sort through the mental fog and analyze the hazy pictures in his head. He was worried about me. Worried that something might happen because of some legend. I wondered what that something might be, so I dug deeper, looking for more. That's when a barrier hit me and I was kicked out of his head.

"Please, don't do that," Aidan said. I didn't even bother to claim I was innocent. He'd see right through the lie. His mind was more or less open to me as much as mine was to his. It could be a helpful tool in finding out whether the other had something to hide, but unfortunately the invasion hardly ever remained undiscovered.

Aidan's fingers wrapped around mine and we walked hand in hand back to the house. I expected him to want to go inside and resume his work, but he lingered in the backyard, intent to watch the sun rise. We hadn't done that together ever since the morning after the Shadow ritual and my consequent turning, which was also the morning Aidan got to see the bright rays spilling in through the window for the first time in five hundred years.

I raised my gaze to the horizon now streaked with orange and gold. The dark rainclouds from last night had dissipated, leaving behind a clear sky. In spite of the warm rays, the rosebushes climbing up the wall to the first floor were still covered by a thick layer of frost that would thaw at its leisure. Ever since coming here, I had the strange feeling the nature in the Scottish Highlands followed its own pace, as though it had a will of its own.

Taking a deep breath, I let the scent of damp earth and firewood invade my nostrils, then turned to look at Aidan. His dark eyelashes cast moving shadows across his cheeks, making his eyes sparkle like sapphires. The usual morning stubble had appeared on his cheeks and chin. I rose on my toes and rubbed my thumb over the delicate skin, marveling at the tingling sensation it sent down my spine. His gaze swept over me, lingering a tad too long over my lips, and then he smiled. I held my breath at the array of emotions washing over me.

Something was going on and he was scared.

I knew that much already. Aidan was the worrying kind anyway, but I had never seen him so absorbed and out of touch with everything that was going on in my life. I wondered whether that legend about the three forces fighting to gain supremacy had more to it than he let on the other day.

"I wish you'd share it with me," I whispered. His gaze hardened. A moment later, he looked away, signaling me I wasn't going to get any answers from him. He was locking me out of his world again, and I had no idea what else to say to make him realize he could trust me. I was his mate. It was his duty to stop keeping secrets from me because he was harming our bond. Not to mention the curiosity was killing me. Okay, I might have one or two secrets of my own, but I vowed to tell him the moment my problem was solved. On another note, it wasn't like I didn't *try* to talk to him about the haunting, Angel and the strange feeling in the pit of my stomach. It wasn't my fault he wouldn't listen, which could only mean his secret was more serious than mine.

He cupped my face with his big hands and rubbed his thumb against my cheek as his intense gaze bore into me. "You know what we have is special, right?"

I nodded, unable to avert my gaze from his stunning blue eyes that seemed to catch the bright rays of the rising sun.

"Good," he whispered. "Then trust me on this one. You're my bonded mate, Amber. We're meant to be together forever. I won't let anything happen to you or our bond."

"I love you," I whispered, my throat choked with emotion.

"I love you too," he whispered back a moment before he lowered his lips to lock them with mine in a tender kiss. It was over way too soon. When he pulled back, I ran the tip of my tongue over my lips to savor the delicious sensation he left behind and prolong the moment.

"There's something I need to tell you," I began. He cocked a brow but remained silent. I drew a sharp breath, wondering where to even begin. "The haunting the other day—"

He pressed a finger against my lips to silence me. "Amber, stop freaking yourself out by constantly thinking about the prize. You'll see, once you stop thinking about it you'll forget it's even there."

I nodded because his words made sense. Maybe I was freaking out since I couldn't stop thinking about being able to see ghosts. However, that didn't mean I hadn't seen something inside his house. And then there was the other matter.

"Something's wrong with me. I feel different, like—" I stopped to gather my words.

"You're a newly turned vampire. It's perfectly normal to feel strange because your body works differently now. You're no longer weak or restrained by a mortal body's needs."

"That's not what I meant." I shook my head. "You don't understand. Something weird's going on. Like I'm not me and I've no idea what to do about it."

He grabbed my hand and pulled me into his arms. I nestled against his broad chest and inhaled his scent, ready to dump all my worries onto his shoulders.

"It's okay. Don't worry about it. Adjusting to being a vampire takes time," Aidan said. "I remember the first few months after my brother's turning. He was a walking nightmare who had absolutely no control over his urges. He basically couldn't decide whether to make out with a girl or suck her dry. It wasn't pretty. Next to him, you're a saint."

The guy had no idea what he was talking about, but he always knew how to make me feel better. It was one of the many things I loved about him.

"Do you need to get back to your job?" I asked.

He nodded. "But not before you tell me what you were doing inside the shed."

"Ain't happening. A girl's got to keep it interesting by not revealing everything about her."

"Then I'll have to kiss you until you spill out your big secret." His fingers tensed around my waist. I shrieked with pleasure at the outlook of a hundred kisses raining down on my neck, which we liked to call a kissing attack. He raised his brows, amused. "Babe, you know I'll find out eventually, right?"

"Just as much as I'll find out what you're up to." I smiled at the mischievous hint in his eyes, taking him up on the challenge. He had no idea what he was up against. Basically, I wasn't known as the female version of Sherlock Holmes for nothing.

"Come on. Let's go back. I don't want you to freeze to death." He was back in his usual overprotective role. Apparently, the fact that I was a strong and immortal vampire completely slipped his mind. There were times when I doubted he'd ever see more in me than the seventeen-year-old klutz of a girl who used to trip over her own shadow.

"Old habits die hard," I muttered under my breath.

"Huh?"

I shook my head. "Nothing."

He offered me his hand. I grabbed it and accompanied him back to the house, already planning my next move.

Chapter 15

As expected, we barely reached the door when Aidan announced he had to leave that instant. Slowly, his mysteriousness was beginning to tick me off because a.) as my boyfriend he was bound to his duty to spend time with me, and b.) he never ever left without making out with me. In fact, what boyfriend just disappears without using the opportunity as a great excuse for some major snogging? It definitely isn't natural male behavior.

My suspicion raised, I slipped into a black jacket with a high collar behind which I could hide my face if need be, and focused on our bond. He was at the Lore court—I could sense that much. Since I was in Scotland and the place was in London, I couldn't just march over there, so I had to put my teleporting skills to use. The usual sense of nausea overwhelmed me, making my head reel and all color drain from my face,

172

if there was any left, what with being dead and all now. Mind, my still latent vampire abilities were nothing to boast about, but I managed to get a blurred picture of an underground and a foul smell, which was enough for my imagination to conjure the image. I closed my eyes and prepared for the tiny impact against the barrier of time and space that always made my heart skip a beat. The usual vortex sucking me in told me I was no longer master of my body or mind, but a scattered presence in the endless pool of cosmic awareness. A moment later, it was over. When I opened my eyes again I found myself in a rundown courtyard surrounded by a barbwire fence and lots of litter on the dusty asphalt.

I took a deep breath and almost choked on the exhume fumes and the scent of rotten garbage. Ah, London—the smell of my worst teenage memories. Before moving to Inverness to work for Aidan, I had lived in a tiny, overpriced basement room with bad lighting and security bars on the window. It had been okay because I didn't know any better, but now, after weeks of breathing in clean air and living in a spacey mansion, I wouldn't be caught dead visiting my old neighborhood—no pun intended.

Aidan was somewhere around here, but I had no idea which way to go. The courtyard seemed empty as far as I could see. Coming from somewhere behind the wall to my right, the sweet scent that had been lingering on Aidan lately wafted past, which made me believe I was close to the Lore court. I wondered what the succubi looked like, but I didn't dare waste any time. Aidan, with his perfect teleporting ability, could already be miles away, so I focused my attention back to the task at hand: spy on him.

The narrow staircase with dark, damp walls led underground. Not exactly my favorite direction in the world. In fact, being underground, caged in by darkness, always made me feel like I was stuck in a coffin. Imagine being caught alive—or dead—in that freakishly polished wooden case with nothing but a few pillows to talk to. I shivered at the morbid thought and headed down the stairs anyway, careful not to breathe in too deeply so I wouldn't throw up all over the place.

Darkness became more impenetrable the deeper I descended. Even though it wasn't a steep decline and in no way tiring, I huffed and puffed, probably to feel as though I wasn't completely alone in this narrow space. At some point I thought I heard water dripping, but when I strained my ears to listen the sound was gone again. At least half an hour must've passed when I finally made out a tiny light in the distance. Turning a corner into a wide hall with marble floors, I stopped in my tracks when my glance caught movement coming from above my head. Where I expected decorations was the most frightening ceiling I had ever seen in my life.

"What the heck?" I whispered frozen to the spot as I stared at the hideously contorted bodies with blood dripping from countless gory wounds, reaching out to me as they rubbed their naked skin against each other. A woman's bony fingers kept prodding a man's gashes, making him open and close his toothless mouth like a fish pulled out of the water. His hooded eyes looked hazy, and for a moment I wasn't sure whether he was experiencing ecstasy or pain. Or maybe he was high on both. Either way, it was just sick. I couldn't turn away from the disturbing image fast enough when a finger trailed down my neck, sending a shiver down my spine.

"I haven't seen you before." The female voice was soft and melodious, filled with something I couldn't immediately pinpoint.

Damn. My worst nightmare was coming true. Now that someone discovered my presence, it was only a matter of time until they called Aidan. Not that I feared him, but he was very good at giving the silent treatment and making me feel guilty. I spun around with a surprised smile on my face and took in the brunette with glossy hair reaching down to her narrow waist. The nearly see-through skirt barely covering her modesty looked like it had shrunk in the wash. Her sleeveless tube top didn't give a better impression. My gaze wandered to her full lips painted in thick red that clashed with her porcelain skin. In spite of the tart outfit, she was stunning and I couldn't help the pang of jealousy creeping up on me. If Aidan was hanging out at this place in the company of women like this one, it was no surprise he wouldn't want to spend time with me. Cosmo always says jealousy isn't an attractive trait in any female, but can you blame me? Even if it weren't for the woman's sultry lips, the unspoken promises of pleasure mirrored in her eyes signaling she was up for *anything*, her outfit didn't fail to convey the message. I couldn't compete with *that*.

"We met a while back. Just changed my hair color and lost a bit of weight. Nothing major but I still get that 'oh-my-gosh-what-happened-to-you' all the time." I laughed nervously, wondering whether I had always been such a bad liar.

"Are you looking for anyone in particular? Maybe I can help." She raised her beautifully shaped brows meaningfully.

My heart began to hammer in my chest. It was a hint that she knew about Aidan and wouldn't hesitate to spill the beans on me. My brain kicked into motion as it tried to come up with various exit strategies.

Teleport out of here? Might work but Aidan would still find out about my unexpected visit, and I wasn't so great at denying facts. In fact, I'd probably end up confessing before he even asked.

Pretend I had lost my way? She might just insist on accompanying me out of this weird subterranean building and probably ask lots of questions in the process. Again, my lying abilities were just as lacking as my supernatural skills.

My best bet was to pretend I was someone else. But who wasn't at least five foot seven and wouldn't be around for months, if not years?

Cass.

By the time my brother married her and she was finally free of her curse, the whole stunt would be long forgotten, you know, water under the bridge. But could I really pull it off?

I raised my head a notch and imagined what cocky Cass would do in such a situation. "Some guy hooked me up with the ambassador position. Thought I'd take a look at this dump before I make up my mind." I cringed inside at how fake I sounded.

"Then you must be Cassandra, the new ambassador. What a pleasure, Your Highness. I'm Persephone, your personal servant." She bowed deeply until her hair brushed the marble floor.

I smiled, getting into it, and waved my hand to signal she may rise. "Nah, I don't need a personal servant when I have the entire Hell at my disposal." My gaze swept over her perfect features and slightly parted lips. "But you can do something for me. I have reason to believe a vampire was here. Tall, dark hair, blue eyes." I hoped I didn't sound too gushy. "He isn't my type at all, by the way."

Persephone inched a step closer to whisper in my ear. "I'm not usually at disposal to disclose who our visitors are, but I'm sure Layla would want me to make an exception for the Princess of Darkness. The vampire, Aidan, came to talk with Layla, then left again. Maybe half an hour ago."

Damn. I must've arrived after he left, meaning I must've missed him by minutes. My teleporting abilities sucked big time.

"Are you looking for him?" Persephone's inquiring voice jolted me out of my thoughts. I shrugged, hoping it was something Cass would do in such a situation. Persephone licked her upper lip slowly as her eyes met mine. "I know where he is, and if you give me a few minutes of your time, I'll tell you." Her long fingers with perfectly manicured nails trailed up the sleeve of my jacket.

My eyes grew wide as realization kicked in. Whoa, was she hitting on me? It couldn't be and yet the way she regarded me from under half-closed lids, and kept licking her lips made it impossible not to get the message. I jumped a step back to put some much-needed distance between us. "Don't get your hopes up. I play for the other team, mate."

"I can be whatever you want me to be." Her features changed from soft femininity to hard masculinity. Her hair shortened to a fashionable bedhead that brushed her naked shoulders. Her lips remained sultry and luscious but her chin became more pronounced, conveying a sense of stubbornness and virility. Even her tiny skirt changed into tight pants that didn't leave much to the imagination. She smiled self-assured. "Still don't like me?"

I cocked my head to the side, wondering why Aidan didn't tell me beings like her existed. It would've made for great dinner conversation. "Can you also change into a bear or a wolf?"

For a brief second, an irritated frown crossed Persephone's smooth forehead. "We can only take one male and one female form. Why? Don't you like me? I could call a few friends of mine so you can have your pick." She took another step forward and I realized the succubus had no immediate intention to give up. As much as I was up for a chat, I had wasted a lot of time already.

"The vampire—" I infused a sharp tone into my voice "—where is he?"

She pouted as her appearance changed from male back to female. "Wembley High Street."

"What's on Wembley High Street?" I asked, confused. That part of London wasn't really known for much, unless Aidan was looking to buy fruit and vegetables from the countless Asian markets that sold fresh produce at a fragment of retail prices. Given that he was a vampire, I was pretty sure there had to be another purpose for his visit.

"There's an antiques shop that's supposed to have something Aidan's looking for," Persephone said. I flicked through my memories of Wembley, mentally walking down the main street as I tried to remember each and every shop I used to frequent for bargains. Just as I thought there was no antiques shop, my mind conjured the image of a tiny door squeezed in between a cash automat and the huge shop window of a clothes retailer. Could it be it? My excitement grew as I focused on the picture in my head.

"Cheers," I said, slapping Persephone's rounded shoulder absentmindedly. The touch sent a jolt through my body, making me lose my breath for a tiny moment, but other than that her presence did nothing for me. Her eyes widened with surprise, as though she, too, wondered why her succubus touch wasn't sending me into pleasure heaven like Aidan predicted it would. Maybe I wasn't as ordinary as I thought. Maybe I had some sort of inborn immunity.

"Don't worry about it," I said. "I'm pretty sure the next person walking down that staircase will trip over themselves to get a date with you. You know the saying, you win some, you lose some." I shot her a smile and closed my eyes, summoning the picture of the tiny door in my mind. An instant later, I felt tiny droplets splattering my skin, so I opened my eyes.

Wembley High Street greeted me with the usual influx of mid-morning buyers hitting the busy shops. Rows of honking cars and double-decker buses crowded the narrow street as travellers, hurrying to and from the subway station, squeezed in between rather than walk the short distance to a crossing.

In the last few weeks, I thought I missed the commotion of city life but, standing here at rush hour, I realized I couldn't get this over and done with fast enough so I could finally return to the tranquility of my new home.

* * *

With its scratched metal frame and scrubby fingerprints on the glass, the door to the antiques shop blended right in with the bleak, concrete building. A brass tag advertised the name, HORST & Co., which sounded as nondescript as the store looked, revealing nothing about what hid behind. For a whole three seconds I considered my options. Of course I could just march in there and use the surprise moment to demand that Aidan tell me what was going on. While that was the kind of strategy you could normally expect from me, I wasn't so sure it'd work with a guy like Aidan. Keeping guard outside until Aidan walked out with his purchase sounded like the better plan. For all I knew Aidan might already be gone, but I figured it was a risk worth taking.

I crossed the street and hid behind the clear wall that shielded customers from the British wind and rain as they waited for their bus. The traffic lights changed from green to red and then back to green a few times before I felt a slight tremor in the air. A moment later, the shop door opened and a tall guy walked out. Even though the collar of his black leather coat was pulled up to hide half of his face, I wouldn't mistake him in million years. His hair was dark and shiny; his eyes were of an unnatural shade of blue. Clutched to his chest was a brown bundle, almost as large as a paperback book, tied together with brown strings. I cocked my head and focused to get a better glimpse when he turned his head, as though sensing my presence. I ducked back down. My heart hammered in my chest, drowning out the traffic noise. His glance remained focused in my direction.

For a brief second, I was terrified he had seen me. But then he turned his back on me, and a moment later he disappeared before everyone's eyes. If people noticed his teleporting, no one reacted in any way. No one fainted or screamed. I wondered how he did that.

Breathing out relieved, I got up to head for the antiques shop when I bumped into someone's strong chest.

Chapter 16

Shielding my eyes from the bright morning sun, I looked up slowly, my mind already working on emergency mode to come up with a good excuse as to why I was in Wembley, watching an antiques shop from across the street. As usual, the kind of excuses my brain came up with wouldn't even convince a child. Luckily for me, the person staring at me wasn't Aidan.

"Hey. Trying to meet your five a day? You don't look like a fresh-fruit kind of guy." I shot Devon a hesitant smile. While I was thrilled that I wouldn't need to try to lie to Aidan yet again, my heart still picked up in speed. Devon was my enemy, and now I was on my own with no magic-infused gate to keep me safe. I didn't even know what this guy's abilities were, which seemed to be a well-kept secret in the Shadow world. So I had to be careful.

He heaved a big sigh. "What are you doing here, Amber?"

Yeah, I got that question a lot lately. If I didn't know any better, I might just start to think people didn't want me around. My smile widened as I pointed at our surroundings. "Why, the same thing as you. I'm enjoying a bit of British culture and natural produce."

He smiled but it didn't reach his eyes. "You shouldn't be here. It's dangerous."

"What could possibly be dangerous about Wembley during the week in broad daylight? Unless you're talking about carrots. I've heard they're not as good for you as everyone claims."

"Come on." He held out his hand. I hesitated for a second before letting him help me up. "Wanna get a cup of coffee with me?"

He was kidding, right? I regarded him from under my lashes. "Does blowing into it count?"

"Sorry, I forgot." He seemed genuinely upset now and I couldn't help but feel I didn't hold the same value for him I once had when my body could still be run over by a car or die of a heart attack. For some reason it bothered me even though it shouldn't. I decided to change the subject. "I used to live about half an hour from here."

His expression lighted up instantly, as though he actually cared to find out more about me. "Really?"

I nodded. "Yep. I moved out at sixteen, rented a room and got a part-time job after school. Every

Saturday, I'd pop over to the market in Alperton and stock up for the week."

"Why didn't you live with your parents?"

"I just didn't." My eyes shifted to the dirty asphalt, avoiding his probing gaze. How could I tell him that I didn't want to be a burden to my poor parents? After my father's illness, all our money went to various doctors trying to cure him. When he finally beat the disease, they were up to their necks in debt. I figured they'd done so much for me already, they were in big financial trouble. So both Dallas and I grew up quickly and started our own lives.

Devon's hand wrapped around my fingers and gave them a gentle squeeze. "If you ever feel like talking, I've been told I'm a good listener."

I nodded, even though I was convinced I'd never tell him. Not even Aidan knew and I liked to keep it that way. "The café over there's quite good." I pointed across the street to a gray building with huge glass windows and a red banner advertising a midday deal. "Can you enter?"

"You mean whether I can step over the threshold without an invitation?" A spark of amusement appeared in Devon's black eyes.

I shrugged. "You need an invite to enter Aidan's property."

He tucked at my arm gently as we crossed the street. "That's because your boyfriend knows what's harmful to a Shadow. The invitation part applies to vampires only. Didn't you watch *Dracula*?"

I could tell he was joking by the way the corners of his lips twitched. "Might've missed that one."

"I have it on DVD. Maybe you could come over to my place and watch it with me some time." His tone was friendly and nonchalant. Harmless. But I knew there was nothing harmless about Devon, or the place where he resided.

"You're hitting on me." I dared a small smile as Devon pushed the door open to the café and waited until I walked past him.

"Are you surprised? You kissed me."

"It was just a peck on the cheek." I moistened my lips, avoiding his gaze. He had tried to flirt with me before. At that time I figured he was only interested in my ability to talk with the dead. I retrieved the Book of the Shadows for his kind, so they had no more use for me. And particularly not now that I was his enemy—and that I had a boyfriend who, needless to say, was his century-old foe. I had no idea what to make of him.

"Don't worry," Devon said. "I'm not going to be all over you in the hope of convincing you that you're dating the wrong person. You'll recognize that part soon enough. Why don't you take a seat? I'll be right back."

I sat down at a nearby table and regarded Devon's back as he instructed the barista. From behind he looked so similar to Aidan: tall with broad shoulders and dark hair that brushed the collar of his jacket. I found him attractive, but I didn't feel the chemistry. Or did I?

A loud bang echoed in my ears, and for a moment everything blacked out like someone switched off the lights. It didn't last long, anything between a few seconds and a minute or two. When my vision returned and I finally resurfaced, I was sitting in my chair propped against Devon's chest. He was whispering something. It took me a while to realize it was a foreign language I didn't recognize.

Groaning, I shifted in my seat to bring a few inches between us, and rubbed my neck. My heartbeat was steady, but the fog inside my head didn't seem to want to dissipate. "What did you say?"

He looked taken aback, like he didn't expect the question. "You were unresponsive." He pushed a cup of coffee in front of me as though that'd answer my question.

Thanks," I said, wrapping my hands around the hot beverage, itching to take a sip.

He inched forward until I could feel his warm breath on my lips. "Your eyes are flickering."

"That's a horrible pickup line. You should've tried 'sparkle like diamonds'."

He frowned. "No, Amber. Your eyes have changed color to red and purple."

"Oh." I peered around me only now realizing I didn't bother to bring my handbag with my compact mirror, so I picked up a knife to regard myself. My reflection was blurred but I noticed something blood red that seemed to shift as I moved my eyes. "Crap. Not again."

"It happened before?"

He made it sound like I was at the doctor's complaining about a rash or sore throat. Irritated, I dropped the knife on the table and turned to face him, ready to change the subject because I sure had no explanation up my sleeve. "How's your coffee? Good? Care to describe what it tastes like because right now I'd kill for a single sip."

"I get it, you don't wanna talk about it." He nodded and gulped down half of his coffee, making me instantly jealous. "It's delicious with a strong yet smooth aroma. Is that a hint of vanilla? I swear I ordered cinnamon but vanilla's even better."

I slapped his hand lightly. "Shut up. You're so not helping."

"So, you're in big trouble, huh?" He put the cup down as his gaze met mine again. And this time I could see an intensity there that worried me. I felt like a tiny mouse watched by the big hawk. Should I deny it? Part of me knew that was the right thing to do. When the hawk's waiting for the precise moment to attack, you don't share with him your weakness. I opened my mouth to tell him he had it all wrong when he interrupted me. "Is that why you called Brendan? You thought he could help you?"

I hated how horribly weak and useless that made me sound. "It was the other way round, but we came to an understanding," I blurted out before I could stop myself.

"What did he want?" Something shimmered in Devon's eyes. I stared at that blackness, allowing it to suck me in. Damn, me and my big mouth. My mind went blank an instant before a sense of peace and trust and tranquility washed over me.

The guy was messing with my head.

He was trying to use me again, just the way he did a few weeks ago.

"Why don't you ask him? Or better yet, see whether you can screw with his mind as well. He might appreciate it more than I do." Getting up, I kicked my chair aside and headed for the door. He caught up with me outside the café as I was about to teleport in front of a huge crowd that was so typical of Wembley. Devon's hand wrapped around my upper arm, and I stopped, but not because I wanted to. If I teleported now, I'd take him with me, and that was the last thing I needed.

"I'm sorry," he whispered. "Old habits die hard. But I swear I didn't mean to. I just worry about you."

A very *un*lady-like snort escaped my throat. "Yeah, right. Like the giant hawk you are."

"Huh?"

I waved my hand in his face. "Forget it. I was planning to tell you, but now I'm not going to."

"Amber, I'm really sorry." He took a deep breath. I strained to read his expression. He wanted to know my secret badly; I could see it in the way his brows furrowed slightly yet he tried hard to relax, as though it didn't matter. But it did. "Brendan's still young," Devon continued. "He doesn't know what he's doing." So, it wasn't about me but Brendan. "If you tell me what he wanted, I'll tell you what Aidan was doing here. That's why you went to the Lore court, isn't it?"

I shivered as images of Devon following me like a creep flashed before my eyes. "How do you know?"

He shrugged. "Just because your boyfriend leaves you unsupervised to visit that place doesn't mean I won't take care of you. Do you have any idea what could've happened to you? That place is dangerous. A touch from that succubus, and you could've been lost forever."

I lifted my chin a notch, ready to jump to Aidan's defense if need be, but Devon didn't pursue the matter.

"Do we have a deal?" he asked.

"No deal. I don't need you to reveal Aidan's secret when I can just ask him myself."

He laughed softly. "Really? Is that why you need to spy on him? Because he's so *open* and honest with you?" The guy sure knew how to make my relationship sound like a giant soap opera with everyone deceiving everyone else. But he did have a point. How many times did I ask Aidan and he refused to tell me? Here was my chance to find out what was going on. I pondered over my options. Go home and forget about it. Knowing my inability to keep my nose out of other people's affairs, that wouldn't work in a million years. Or I could just take Devon up on his offer. What was the harm in telling him what Brendan wanted? They had this weird blood-thing going on, so it was probably just a matter of Brendan not wanting to burden him. In a twisted kind of way, my logic actually made sense to me.

"Okay—" I took a deep breath "—but you go first." Devon shook his head. I rolled my eyes. "Oh, come on. What's with the trust issues? I wasn't the one who kidnapped you!"

"We only tried to protect you."

If he kept saying that every time I brought up the issue, I might just end up slapping him. I didn't need protection from a guy. Not in the past, present or future. "I'll give in, but only because I want to get back home before Aidan realizes I'm gone. Brendan came to tell me about Angel's disappearance." It was half the truth, but Devon needn't know. I was proud of myself that I didn't stumble over my words. In fact, I was slowly getting really good at this telling-only-half-the-truth thing. And then I figured if I kept half the stuff to myself, he might just do the same to me.

"Is that all? He said nothing else?" Devon's tone raised my suspicion. There was more to the whole story, I knew that part straight away. This was my chance to find out what that was.

"Obviously not." I scoffed. "There's something fishy about the whole affair. It's pretty obvious someone she trusted persuaded her to go with them.

Maybe she was threatened. Obviously, Brendan is hell bent on finding out what happened and I think I can help."

Devon didn't even blink. The way he just kept staring in silence with an unreadable expression on his face made me feel uncomfortable. "You think someone threatened her?"

Whoa, was he asking me for *my* opinion? I shrugged. "Does it matter? A dear friend is gone and I won't rest until the puzzle is solved."

"So, what have you found out so far?" His eyes glittered unnaturally bright. I could feel something in the air. Maybe apprehension. Was he nervous? Did he think I had discovered something I shouldn't have? My heartbeat sped up. Granted, I never figured I might just be a natural-born Sherlock Holmes, but I couldn't ignore the facts. I had a new lead, and this time it was Devon. He knew something that Brendan didn't, that consequently I didn't. I only had to find out what that something was.

"Well—" I moistened my lips slowly "—let's just say it's big. I had no idea it was this huge and so many people are involved."

A frown appeared on his forehead. "A conspiracy?"

"Yeah, you could say that." I nodded, wide-eyed.

"Did you know your boyfriend and the Lore Court are involved?"

Devon's question took me by surprise. Of course I kind of guessed something was going on and Aidan knew more than he let on, but having my suspicion confirmed didn't make it any easier to swallow.

"You didn't," Devon said, misinterpreting my silence. "But surely you wondered why he's been gone so much lately." He inched closer to whisper in my ear. His hot breath brushed my cheek, making me flinch just a little. It was strange but not unpleasant, almost like some part of me enjoyed it, which didn't make any sense. I had absolutely no romantic interest in this guy, and yet...A craving awoke inside me, starting out as a tiny pang, no bigger than maybe a passing fancy that slowly turned into a longing sensation. It took my breath away. My knees began to shake beneath me as my vision blurred and strange pictures flashed through my mind.

A carriage hurried past, the sound of the horse's hooves carrying through the silence of the night. Devon dressed in black from head to toe, his black hair swaying in the wind, his jaw set as he regarded a motionless bundle on the floor. He poked the bundle with the tip of his boot, and then tossed the coarse, gray blanket aside to reveal the bloodless body beneath. And in that instant I knew the killing had been my doing.

I shook my head. Not my doing. The murderer had to be someone else because I wasn't even born yet. A soft laughter echoed in my ear and the pictures returned.

A woman with red curls that reached down to her waist was watching him from the high tower of a church. Her hands were drenched in blood, just like the front of her blue corsage dress. She pressed a perfumed handkerchief against her mouth to get rid of the stench wafting from the streets below and took a step back, disappearing in the shadows. For a moment, my vision shifted and I thought I saw the world through her eyes: running through the busy streets of Victorian London. Killing an innocent just to see his blood staining the dirty cobblestones, all the while thinking of Devon and how sweet his blood would taste.

My stomach clenched, jerking me back to reality. A strong shiver ran down my spine. I knew that woman. It was Aidan's ex, Rebecca. She had known Devon, followed him even, but why? She could've easily attacked him if she only sought his blood. But she wanted more. Did she have a crush on him?

And why would I think I was her?

I had to clear my throat several times before I found my voice again. "I told you what I know. Now it's time to keep your part of the bargain."

"My pleasure." Even though I couldn't read his expression because his mouth still lingered an inch from my ear, I knew he was smiling, as though he expected me to dump Aidan after I discovered his secret. I instantly prepared myself for the worst. "Aidan's been frequenting the Lore court for a while, but not as much as he has in the last few days since he accepted a job for Layla." That much I knew already. While I didn't like the bitch hitting on him, I couldn't ask him to give up his job. I nodded so Devon would continue. "Layla fears someone's about to take over her throne and Aidan's supposed to find the person. Trouble is he hasn't been able to locate him yet."

When he stopped I peered up at him, relieved but also a bit disappointed. "Is that your big revelation? Boy, you just dropped a bomb. I don't even know where to start picking up the pieces."

Devon smiled. "Not quite, Amber. Don't you want to know what she offered him in return for his services?" Did I want to know that? Not really, but I nodded anyway. "The whereabouts of a mirror that can fuse any soul with a mortal body. Does the name Rebecca ring any bells?"

A mirror.

I had found one at the shed a few minutes before Aidan arrived. He never told me what he came for, just took me home with the pretense to come back later. All blood drained from my face. I felt so faint I thought I might just drop to the ground and die there and then. Rebecca, the crazy ex who turned him into a vampire. Granted, she was pretty with red hair, gorgeous eyes and skin as smooth as alabaster. But what the heck? She was a bitch. Had he lost his marbles? Got the crazies? What guy in his right mind wanted to date a psycho killer? Was the blood bond between Aidan and her so strong he simply couldn't let her go? Or did his feelings go deeper than he claimed?

It certainly explained why he took Layla's job and wouldn't tell me anything about it. I knew all along he had something to gain, now I also knew what.

I took a deep breath as I tried to push the array of questions to the back of my mind. There'd be enough time to think about them later after I kicked his ass into next week. Good that I hadn't slept with the cheater yet.

"Did you know Aidan's house is haunted?" I laughed at his perplexed expression. "Yeah, me neither until a few days ago when blood started to spill down the walls and scratches began to appear on the floor."

"Are you sure?"

"As sure as any necromancer could be." I regarded him intently. "Why? You don't believe me?"

"Of course I believe you. Are you okay?" Judging from his tone, he was telling the truth.

"Oh, you bet I am. It's just a ghost." I waved my hand in the air. "All it can do is walk through some walls and wail in its nightgown, right?"

Devon nodded, seemingly unconvinced. "If you need anything—" His voice trailed off.

"Nah, unless you can find me a coffin, and preferably one Aidan won't be able to pry open because I intend to send him on a very long date with a ghost." I smiled sweetly. "Thanks for an interesting day. I had fun."

"So did I." His face inched closer. The air crackled. Time seemed to stand still. I held my breath, almost expecting—fearing—he might kiss me. Even though I was pissed at Aidan, I didn't feel like kissing another guy. To my relief, Devon leaned in to plant a soft peck on my cheek, lingering just a tiny bit but long enough to allow me to take a whiff of his aftershave. I breathed in, surprised how much I liked it.

"I'll call you." My voice came lower than planned, full with promises I had no intention to keep.

"I hope so," Devon said before he began walking down the street.

His departure came so sudden, I stared after him until he disappeared in the mass of people, towering at least a head over them. Only when I could no longer see his dark hair and broad shoulders did I teleport back to Scotland, more furious than I had ever been in my entire life.

Chapter 17

I materialized in the backyard next to the wilted rosebushes. I was able to let my anger roam free for all of three seconds, or as long as it took to kick the garden bench, sending it flying through the air a few feet, after which I regained my composure. I even managed a tiny smile even though I probably looked like a psycho, but who cared? I was an enraged woman on a mission.

So here's what I did when I arrived home. Even though every single cell inside my body screamed to toss one vase after another over Aidan's head, I didn't enter the mansion straight away because I was an adult in a grownup relationship so, consequently, I was going to defy my nature and actually talk things over. He deserved a chance to explain himself.

I tapped a finger against my lips, thinking.

Maybe talking wasn't such a bright idea. The guy would just end up denying everything and we'll live happily ever after...until he managed to raise his crazy ex.

So a trap it was.

But how would I go about things? Obviously, checking his emails and wiring his phone calls wouldn't work, what with her being dead and probably not having cell phone reception in Hell, where she belonged. I could also scratch the other obvious things like GPS logger, going through his browser history, or the girl trap—Aidan wasn't so stupid as to fall for the 'hot chick chatting him up in a bar' technique that was about as old as humanity.

A voice-activated recorder would record everything he said on his cell phone while driving because, in the case of an affair, a working vehicle's a necessary tool in his deceptions. In my case, I could use it record any monologues if he talked into thin air, thinking his dead beloved was listening. Trouble might be figuring out where to hide it so he wouldn't find out. A teddy bear concealing the nanny cam might just be too obvious with an overly careful guy like Aidan.

The excitement of having come up with a plan wore off pretty soon. The recorder idea wasn't bad but, all in all, my options were slim and not exactly reliable. Let's be honest, except for the few tidbits I picked up reading Cosmo, I had no real-life experience with catching cheaters. I began to chew my nails as I realized I needed to talk to a pro. Preferably someone who was a master at disguising the truth, and who might be a better choice than Cass? After her stunt with Dallas during which she made him believe he was about to die and the only way to enter Heaven was to marry her, I had yet to decide whether to be shocked or amused. The girl had a great deal of imagination, I had to give her that. But she also couldn't keep her mouth shut if her life depended on it.

Call her or not call her?

I had nothing to lose so I fished my phone out of my pocket and dialed her number. She picked up on the second ring.

"It took you a week to call. Do you realize how long that is in *Hell*-years?" Cass yelled.

I smiled. "I missed you too. It's so lovely to find you in such a good mood." Slowly counting to ten, I pushed the phone away from my ears as Cass fell into a long tirade of whining in self-pity.

"—and then Dad—" she was talking about Lucifer "—had the cheek to offer Dallas a job. Do you know what that means? Even if he married me, which by the look of it he never will, we'd be stuck down here because Dallas is too scared to tell Dad to shove his job where the sun don't shine."

"Maybe Dallas wants the job. He seemed to get along with your dad just fine."

Cass snorted. "Like a house on fire. Last week Dad showed him the dungeons and *forgot* to bring him back. It took me four hours to find him."

200

I sighed, ready to change the subject before she started recalling more of those incidents that only made me feel bad for both Dallas and my parents. I mean, I should've protected my brother rather than let him get involved in this mess. Our poor parents believed we were having a quiet summer in Scotland and that we'd be home by Christmas. How would I explain that not only was I a vampire now, but Dallas was stuck in Hell after a voodoo priestess returned his soul to his dead body? Talk about perfect dinner conversation. I could picture it all in my head:

Dad: Amber, how was your day?

Me: Great.

Dad, leaning over the table, interested: What did you do?

Me: I went to class and then stopped to grab a bite.

Dad: Sounds fantastic. What did you have?

Me (kicking Dallas' leg under the table so he wouldn't burst out in laughter): Judging from the accent, I think I had something French.

Dad, pointing at my plate: That certainly explains the pecking at your food.

"Hey, are you still there?" Cass yelled in my ear, jerking me out of my thoughts.

"Sure." Cass's inability to stay focused was slowly rubbing off on me. "I meant to ask you about your new abilities."

"They're cool. Wouldn't be bad if I actually were in the real world where I'd have a proper use for them." I nodded even though she couldn't see me. "So, why did you call?"

Her question took me by surprise. "To see how you're doing."

"Of course. What else?" She clicked her tongue. "This pretty face ain't stupid, mate. If you had been interested in my wellbeing, you wouldn't have waited a whole week to inquire about it. Just spill."

"I would've called but so much came up." Even though it was the truth, I cringed at how horribly fake my excuse sounded. "One day we'll sit down and I'll explain everything."

"You bet your ass we will. In fact, I'm free this weekend. You could pop over, maybe even stay the night, you know, girls' night in." Cass only ever invited me twice: to impress Dallas and for her birthday party so I could persuade Dallas to marry her. The girl was clearly in desperate need of *any* contact with the outside world.

"I'd like that," I said, hoping she'd forget about the invitation before the week was over. As much as I loved Cass, I couldn't take the heat down there. Literally. "I meant to ask you something. Let's say this friend of mine suspects her boyfriend might still be hung up on the ex. How would you go about trapping him to find out?"

"Oh!" Tiny pause followed by a giggle, then, "You're talking about this friend of yours called Amber?"

"No," I said slowly. "I'm talking about the other friend called 'it's none of your business, got it?' Now, can we get back to the trapping part, please? What do you suggest?"

"Pretty obvious. Plan a trip out of town, but you're not actually going anywhere, just make him think that you are. This is where you set your trap. If he thinks you're going to be away, then there's a good chance he might use this as an opportunity to meet up with the other chick."

I regarded the leaves on the ground as I took in her advice. Not bad at all...if I didn't leave out one tiny detail. "What if the chick's whacked?"

"You mean like in 'dead'? Doesn't matter. In fact, getting in touch with a corpse is kinda time-consuming and requires a lot of preparation so I'm pretty sure he won't let the opportunity go to waste."

She made it sound as though my boyfriend was indeed cheating on me. "It's not definite. He might not really be cheating on my friend."

"Yeah," Cass said unconvinced. "You know, I should send over one of my most trusted advisors. His name is Kinky and he knows a thing or two about guys."

Kinky? The tiny devil that used to sit on Cass's shoulder to teach her proper Hell etiquette? "Ah, yeah, no!" I laughed. "Unless I wanted a divorce!"

"You mean your friend wanted a divorce."

Damn it. I was the worst liar ever. I couldn't keep my stories straight if they were written across my forehead. "That's what I said."

"I bet you did."

Time to change the subject again. "Cass, do you think kissing another guy on the cheek is cheating?"

"Did you use tongue?" I could hear the amusement in her voice. Eww, what would I use that for? I shook my head as she continued, "It depends on whether the boyfriend in question is Scottish. 'Cause if he is then, according to the Scottish laws of dating, it's second degree cheating. And if the other guy is hot, then it's automatically moving up to first degree."

I didn't know whether to take her seriously or not, but it sure made me feel bad. "Really?"

"Of course not. It was just a peck...unless you harbored lots of naughty thoughts afterwards. Did you?"

"No!" Why did I sound as though I was lying even when I was telling the truth?

"Shame," Cass said. "Wait, you sound guilty."

"I'm not." My answer came out all squeaky and loud.

"Maybe you should since you cheated on him according to Scottish standards. I'll send over Pinky who can help you develop a guilty conscience."

Pinky was the opposite of Kinky, instructed by Cass's seraph mother to teach Cass proper Heaven etiquette. Knowing Cass, that job didn't turn out so well. "No, thanks. I'll call you to let you know how my friend's trap turned out."

"You gotta go already?" She sounded whiny. "Don't forget to call." I felt bad at the disappointment in her voice. I could only imagine how lonely it must be down there in the deep pits of Hell with only a handful of demons as company.

"I won't," I said. "Thanks, Cass. You're the best." I meant every word of it. A minute later, I hung up and took a deep breath before I headed for Aidan's mansion, a plan already forming in my head.

Chapter 18

I entered the house through the backdoor and crossed the marvelous yet unused kitchen in a few long strides. Everything was deserted as usual, which didn't surprise me. I took a shower in my own bathroom to wash off the scent of Devon, the succubus, exhaust fumes, and crowded streets, and put on a pair of jeans and a long sweater, then sat down in the library to wait for Aidan.

My fingers started drumming on my thigh as I counted the seconds until Aidan arrived. The sun set outside in a multitude of colors, bathing the sky in copper and red. Under normal circumstances, nothing could've kept me from enjoying the breathtakingly beautiful view, but I couldn't focus on it tonight. Not when my boyfriend was probably plotting to raise his ex this instant.

It wasn't long before he stormed in and stopped in his tracks, as though he was surprised to see me. His cheeks flushed, giving his skin a pink hue. "You're home."

I cocked a brow. "Isn't that where you told me to be?"

"I did. I was just—" He waved a hand in the air, searching for words.

"Surprised to see I listened?"

He laughed nervously. "There's something I need to finish. I'll be in my study."

"Sure. Take your time." I narrowed my gaze as he walked out. Talk about acting all weird. If he thought I wouldn't try to find out what he was up to, he was in for a big surprise.

After five minutes of tapping my fingers against my thigh to kill time, I tiptoed up the stairs and crept to his office, avoiding the creaking floorboards and the heavy furniture Aidan called 'antiques' while I liked to call them 'dust magnets'.

The door was closed, but my vampire senses were heightened enough to make out muffled sounds. I pressed my ear against the keyhole and held my breath to listen. Aidan was walking up and down the room, the sound of his boots was almost swallowed up by the thick carpet, which suited me just fine because it didn't distract from his conversation.

"No! I want you to stay there until I've sorted out this mess," he whispered. I could tell he was mad but struggling to keep his voice done the way only Aidan could. "Look, there's nothing you can help with. You'd only overcomplicate things and I don't need the distraction right now. Just stay put and I'll get you when it's done so we can commence the gathering. And one more thing, Amber's been very suspicious lately. She doesn't need to know so don't talk to her."

I took a deep breath, hundreds of thoughts racing through my mind. As I figured before, Aidan was keeping a secret from me. Again. But now I was pretty sure this one involved his ex, Rebecca, and he didn't want her ghost to talk to me. I knew all along the guy was too good to be true. Must be running in the family. Just look at Kieran and his tendency to whisper sweet nothings to every woman crossing his path to make them fall in love with him. Once they did, he moved on to the next.

"You're so busted, Mister," I mumbled under my breath as I tiptoed back down the stairs, considering my next step. Of course I could just follow Cass's advice and plant a trap, but there was no need for it any longer. I had all the proof I needed. Obviously, I wouldn't hang around until his psycho ex made her grand appearance. The plan was to help find Angel, and then get the hell out of there. My heart was about to burst from the pain of Aidan's betrayal. A voice inside my head screamed to kick him where it hurt the most. And maybe I would, one day, but right now I needed to focus my mind on my friends who really mattered.

Even though I had already checked the shed in the woods and found nothing but a mirror, I had the strange feeling I missed something. I dashed out the door into the backyard, ready to teleport, when I felt a hand on my back, startling me.

"Whoa," Aidan said. "It's just me. Talk about being engrossed in your thoughts. I hope I was in them."

I smiled weakly as I averted my gaze, ignoring his unspoken question. "Do you need to leave again?"

"You caught me."

Yeah, that wasn't the only thing I caught. "The whole night?" I asked. He ran a hand through his hair as I regarded him. I took that as an affirmative. "It's fine, Aidan. Don't sweat it. I'm busy anyway."

"Thanks, I won't be long. You're the coolest girlfriend ever. I swear I'll make it up to you. What do you say we spend tomorrow evening together? Just the two of us."

I nodded because deep in my heart I couldn't imagine anything that would give me more pleasure. But playing happy couple wasn't the way things would roll from now on.

Aidan kissed me quickly, then dissolved into thin air as I patted my tingling lips. They felt naked, empty, as though Aidan had taken a part of me with him. It was probably this eternal bond we shared that made me love him more than he loved me. Maybe he was immune to it, or his love for Rebecca was stronger. I wanted to fight for him, but was there even a point when Rebecca and he had a history no one would ever be able to erase? Whatever he chose, I only wished him happiness, so I vowed I wouldn't get involved.

Five long minutes later, I closed my eyes and imagined the shed. A tremor shook my body, making my stomach turn. When I opened my eyes again, I was standing on the narrow path leading up to the shed.

The rising moon bathed the trees and leaves in a dark silver, tranquil hue. A strong breeze stirred the fallen leaves on the ground. I took a deep breath of the cool night air and started up the snaking path at a fast pace. I barely reached the shed when my hearing picked up something in the distance. Like the long wail of a—wolf?

I frowned. No, it had to be a dog because, as far as I knew, there were no wolves in Scotland. Maybe someone lost their pet in the wilderness and the poor animal was scared to death. A pang of hunger hit me full force. I groaned. Not again! There was no time to deal with this right now. With a flick of my wrist, I yanked open the door to the shed and entered, ready to give it a more thorough examination than before.

A few minutes later, I still found nothing and the first crumbles of doubt began to nag at me. Maybe my intuition was wrong and Angel wasn't here. Maybe this wasn't the right shed and I was wasting my time when I should've been searching the parameter. Leaving was the reasonable thing to do, yet my legs wouldn't budge. I had never really been the superstitious kind, but I couldn't shake off the feeling there was more to this shed than met the eye. I just couldn't pinpoint what it was or where this knowledge was actually coming from.

I sat down on the ground to think when something stirred outside. Branches scraped the glass of the window and a dark shadow appeared, blocking the moonlight. Holding my breath, I crawled to the far left corner in the hope that whoever was outside wouldn't come in. If they did, I'd teleport my way out of here before anyone noticed my presence. I waited for the door to open, but it didn't. Instead, I recognized Devon's voice.

"I told you he's not here. If the bounty hunter couldn't sense him, then he must've taken her somewhere else."

My brain kicked into motion, putting two and two together. By bounty hunter, Devon probably meant Aidan, which surprised me. I always assumed the Shadows referred to us as bloodsuckers. Devon thought Aidan was looking for someone, which could only mean Aidan hadn't found Seth. A soft wail jerked me out of my thoughts.

"I don't think the vampire knows more than we do." Devon's voice trailed off, as though he meant to say more but decided against it. A second later, my phone vibrated in my pocket, the sound cutting through the silence like a knife.

"Crap," I muttered. The same moment, the door burst open and a black wolf charged in, blocking the moonlight. My heart almost stopped in my chest as a whimper escaped my mouth. Wolf was probably the wrong expression because that thing stood on his hind limbs and, with its huge head and shimmering eyes oozing with intelligence, it looked way more human than I cared to acknowledge. And then I remembered one of my early conversations with Aidan when I asked him whether he ever dated one of those things and he replied he wouldn't because they smelled. I groaned inwardly, still staring at the large creature sniffing the air. "A werewolf? You've got to be kidding me!" What was it with me and my inability to keep away from creatures of the night that shouldn't *exist*?

It all happened too quickly and yet it felt as though a year must've passed. The werewolf raised his head and darted in my direction, flying through the air and jumping horizontally against the wall like some sort of circus acrobat. My mouth went instantly dry. My brain screamed to get the hell out of here, but as usual my feet were glued to the spot, unwilling to listen to my brain's command. Behind the werewolf, someone shouted, "Don't hurt her!" Only then did I realize, my gosh, I probably had 'dinner' written all over me. But I didn't want to be dinner; my limbs weren't doggy snacks. My arm went up to protect my face as I closed my eyes and focused on the first place that came to mind an instant before a gust of bad breath hit me in the face.

I was going to die. This thing was going to shred me to pieces.

My stomach turned, leaving me with a strong need to bend over and spill out my guts. I held my breath so I wouldn't puke all over the place. Seconds ticked by. Nothing happened. Or maybe it all happened so fast I didn't even feel the pain. When I finally dared to open my eyes again, I was surrounded by darkness and a faint musky scent. Something soft brushed my cheek. I swiped my fingers across the floor to feel my way around. My foot bumped against something hard. Clothes and books—and lots of them.

I was sitting inside my cupboard.

That was the one safe place I could come up with? Let's just say that was one secret I'd take to my grave—in the figurative sense since, technically, I was already dead.

Breathing out, I pushed up from my cowering position and, stepping over all my clutter, which I liked to stack underneath my clothes hanging from padded clothes hangers, I exited my cupboard.

The room was bathed in darkness with the only source of light coming from the moon outside the window. I switched on the light to get rid of the ominous shadows cast by the furniture and sat down on my bed as I allowed myself to freak out. But for some inexplicable reason I wasn't as scared as I thought I should be. Maybe the shock had to wear off first.

A werewolf.

I laughed uneasily. Would it be coming for me now that it got hold of my scent? I hoped not because, now that Aidan was about to dump me for his ex, I no longer had the privilege of gold-infused gates to protect me. Come to think of it, I didn't need a guy to take care of me. Even before I was turned into a vampire, the supernaturals had needed *me* to retrieve the Shadows' famous Book of the Dead. But just to make sure, I went down to the library, switched on the computer and typed 'vampire vs. werewolf fight winner' into the *Google* search browser.

The machine whirred for zero point twenty-three seconds before it came up with some four million results. Obviously, I wasn't the only nutter interested in this stuff. I clicked on the first link and groaned. Over sixty per cent thought a werewolf would kick a vamp's ass any time. Dammit! I tried another page and then another until I had to admit my chances were pretty slim. Better refresh my werewolf knowledge then. I was about to start my research when a faint scratch echoed from the window.

Begging my body not to faint, I turned my gaze to the closed window, almost expecting an oversized, extremely hairy head to appear. All I could see was the shimmering moon...and then something else. I nearly lost my breath when I glimpsed a translucent woman floating midair with sunken, glazed eyes, pale skin, thin,...and dead. Definitely dead. My heart hammered harder.

A flicker, and then the ghost appeared again.

I was ready to faint right there on the spot. Get a grip, I told myself as the image dissipated, but my heart continued to race. Would the ghost come back? I didn't know but I was ready and prepared—to dash out of this pretty yet obviously haunted house.

Thank goodness I didn't scream like a little princess, or else one of the others might've heard me, raced to my rescue and I'd end up the laughing stock for a whole month. How could I blame them? Most of the inhabitants of the paranormal world were dead anyway, so they obviously didn't fear the *totally dead* as in those lacking an actual physical body.

First the werewolf, now the ghost. If I didn't do something about what was going on, I might just end up losing my marbles. I sighed and pushed the image of an old lady living in a big, creepy house, surrounded by countless cats, to the back of my mind. If Aidan really dumped me, I knew I had a few good points working for me, like my big, brown eyes and my clear skin. Heck, I could be funny too—or so my friends claimed. But maybe they were just trying to be nice.

Ah, who was I kidding? Being a dead *and* blood craving chick might just not score me any brownie points in the dating world. Not when I was a vampire slash necromancer on the verge of a nervous breakdown.

Chapter 19

The first time I checked the shed, Aidan turned up. My second attempt at looking into Angel's whereabouts didn't turn out as planned either. As I recalled my encounters with Angel and everything that happened so far, I could increasingly feel that the shed was at the heart of the mystery. Slowly I was starting to think that shed was better guarded than Hell, or why else would people keep turning up or follow me so I wouldn't get a chance to investigate for longer than a few minutes? People were trying to keep me away from that place. They thought I was a threat, that I might just unravel their well-kept secrets. Yeah, I really liked that idea. A supernatural tangled web of lies, and I, Amber Reed, was about to dig up the dirt and expose the culprits.

Whatever was coming after me—think hungry werewolf and freaky ghost—I was determined to not give up. Now that I knew about my opponents, I vowed to be more careful and only investigate in the safety of daylight. So I spent the night in front of the computer with the lights switched on, my eyes darting across the room every now and then, so I'd be warned of any signs of a ghostly apparition. My ghost didn't return, and neither did the werewolf, but I knew they would be coming eventually. I was way too close to discovering the truth.

The hours from dusk till dawn couldn't pass fast enough. By sunrise I was fully clothed and clutching a bag that contained my usual emergency kit including a compass, pacing up and down the room, ready to go again. As soon as the first rays of sun seeped through the window, I resumed Mission Investigate Mysterious Shed and teleported to the shed, materializing somewhere at the foot of the hill. My teleporting was slowly getting better but it still felt nauseating and I almost never landed where I was supposed to.

I took a good look at my surroundings before darting up the path leading to the shed, then stopped to listen for any signs of a pursuer. No one was around. Goody. I pushed the door open and entered, making sure to close it behind me.

In the warm morning light, the room looked just like any deserted garden hut with off-white walls and a creaking door. With a quick glance I scanned the small room for any changes. Apart from the large hole in the ground, still filled with mud, there was a thick blanket of dust covering the floor, which I swear wasn't there only a few hours ago when I searched the place.

Kneeling down, I swiped a finger through the dust, then lifted it to my nose to take a sniff. During my time as Aidan's housekeeper, he had spared no effort to help me get accustomed with his *antique* furniture that was the worst dust magnet ever. He had expected me to polish and scrub and then polish some more, so I definitely knew what dust smelled like. In fact, even the thought of it still haunted me in my nightmares. The dust on the floor smelled of nothing, which only raised my suspicion. This wasn't real dust—someone had planted it here so they'd know whether I'd pop over to investigate. Clever, but not clever enough!

I closed my eyes and teleported to the far back of the room, right on top of the chair so as not to leave footprints behind. Granted, standing on a chair in an empty room looked stupid. But who cared? I was a girl on a mission and looking good wasn't my priority. The height gave me an advantage as my gaze scanned the floor. To my chagrin, I found nothing. Not even a single hook hinting at a hidden trapdoor. I was at my wit's end. It was either go home or let people know that I had been here by dabbing into one of my worst fears. Heaving a big sigh, I jumped down from the chair and started swiping my hands across the floor, and even though I knew the dust wasn't real, the knowledge didn't stave off the obligatory sneeze or two.

Half an hour later, I gave up. "Useless," I whispered, fishing the tiny mirror I found in the shed and completely forgot about out of my pocket to regard my unruly hair. Dark smudges stained my face where I had pushed loose strands out of my eyes. I looked tired and defeated, but I was nowhere near giving up.

The rays of sun caught in the mirror and reflected like the beam of a flashlight. In the mirror, I thought I caught a faint mark on the other side of the wall. I turned to look but there was nothing there, so I raised the mirror again and played around until I had the right angle. In its reflection, the signs on the other side of the wall were clearly visible.

Circles and pentagrams. Drawings of what looked like people gathered around an eye that seemed to guard a pyre.

My heart started to race. Raising the tiny mirror higher over my shoulder, I slowly moved backward, my gaze still focused on the creepy writings. It reminded me of a—

"Witch-hunt." My whisper barely made its way out of my throat. I swallowed hard as I tried to memorize the drawings so I could look them up later. The bushes outside stirred. It could either be an animal or someone following me. I pushed the mirror shard inside my back pocket and prepared to leave when an idea struck me. I opened my emergency bag and retrieved my compact mirror. Fidgeting with it, I realized the drawings weren't there in its reflection.

The shard I had found wasn't an ordinary mirror.
Smiling, I closed my eyes and teleported back to
Aidan's mansion.

Chapter 20

In the face of a new discovery, excitement often exceeds the actual importance and magnitude of said discovery, which was the case in my situation. Back at the shed, I thought I cracked the case wide open. At home though, I realized I wasn't really anywhere near finding Angel. In fact, the mysterious drawings had ended up complicating my project even more because now I wasn't just dealing with the case of a possible kidnapping. I also had a possible witch-hunt on my plate.

But this wasn't the Middle Ages. As far as I remembered from history class, they were just ordinary women that did no more than brew a few tea leaves—nothing wrong about that if you ask me—marked as witches and burned alive. I wondered whether in this other world I was recently introduced to, where the impossible became possible, finding circles and pentagrams might indicate there was another group of supernaturals out there I didn't yet know about. First vampires, then Shadows, reapers, demons, angels, werewolves, and now witches and maybe...witch hunters? I shuddered at the possibility of my theory being true.

Who, in this century, would hunt down a witch? After the troubles I went through when I became a necromancer, I figured in the paranormal world the correct answer to the question could be 'pretty much everybody except me'. Come to think of it, I might just be about to join the hunt.

I didn't have time to ponder over my new discovery because my phone vibrated almost as soon as I materialized. I peered at the caller ID. It was the same one calling me at the shed when the phone vibrated, attracting the werewolf's attention. I groaned before I answered.

"What's up, Devon? Miss me already?"

"What did I do this time?" Devon asked.

The shed. The werewolf. Devon telling that killer machine I was friend not foe. I bit my tongue for a second so I wouldn't blurt it all out. No point in letting on I knew it was he walking his pet dog in the middle of the night. "Nothing. It was just a phrase I picked up on TV. I liked the sound of it so I thought—" I trailed off.

"Right. Care to join me outside? We need to talk."

"Sure." I cut off the line and slipped into my coat out of habit as I darted through the front door, down the driveway to the gates in the distance. He was already there, a big frown creasing his forehead. The dark circles beneath his eyes made him look tired, less composed than usual.

"Is Aidan around?" Devon asked.

I shook my head. "Do you really think I'd agree to meet you if he was?"

He looked stunned, as though the thought never crossed his mind, but he didn't comment. "Brendan told me about your *situation*. I want to help."

"Really? Even before I deliver the lost girlfriend? I'm flattered."

He smiled. "I can take you to see Deidre. She could perform the ritual again and free from your bloodlust."

"No."

He raised his brows. "Why? You don't trust her?"

I didn't but that wasn't the reason. "Right after I was turned, I didn't suffer from it. I need to find out what triggered it in the first place."

"Brendan thinks you were touched by something that broke our Queen's magic."

Now he had my attention. I leaned against the gates and grasped the metal rods, my knuckles turning white. "Something touched me? Like a different kind of magic?"

He hesitated. "Maybe. I don't know what could possibly be so strong though."

The metal rods felt cold as ice against my skin. I pulled my hands back when it dawned on me. Aidan used magic-infused gold to keep out the Shadows. If something could ban them, then it might just be strong enough to break the spell. "What about this?" I pointed at the gate. Devon's eyes narrowed a tiny bit. I could see his thoughts mirrored in his face: claim Aidan's magic would never work and risk sounding defensive and petty, or keep the possibility open and risk looking weak? In the end, he decided to cock his head to the side and keep his mouth shut.

I heaved a big sigh as something else dawned on me. Aidan was the only person I knew who owned magic-infused gates. He was also the one who knew where to get this kind of magic. Could he have done something to me to weaken my body so I wouldn't hinder his plans regarding Rebecca? It made so much sense that it actually hurt. I took a deep breath as I focused on Devon, hoping my expression wouldn't betray the turmoil going on inside of me. "Do you know anyone I could ask? Maybe a witch?"

A dark shadow crossed his face and I thought I even saw a tiny flinch. "No, I don't." I instantly knew he was lying. He knew a witch, meaning they existed. And if vampires, werewolves, demons, and witches existed, then what else was out there?

"That's too bad, but thanks anyway." I smiled. "Is there something I can help you with? I'm sure you didn't just offer our assistance because I'm such a pretty face."

"Actually, the pretty face part was my main driving factor—" Smiling, he stopped for effect "—but there's something I meant to ask you. Did Aidan say anything about a mirror?"

The mirror again—probably the same one I was carrying in my back pocket. He made it sound nonchalant, like he didn't really care. But I could feel his blood pumping hard through his veins as his heartbeat spiked. Pretending to think, I tapped a finger against my lips. "No, I don't think so. But he's been gone forever lately. I think he's discovered something."

Devon's expression softened a little. "Let's hope he has." Another lie. The guy obviously didn't want Aidan to find that mirror. I wondered whether anyone knew about the secret painted on the shed's walls.

"I gotta go back," I said. "I promised my brother to call him. He's probably worried sick by now."

"That's a funny choice of words. Why would he be worried? You're a strong vampire and a pretty clever one at that." The way he said 'vampire' made my stomach churn. For a moment, I thought I heard contempt in his tone, but it couldn't be because Devon was smiling. It didn't make sense.

"Thanks." I took a step back when I caught movement coming from the trees on my right side.

It was a huge, familiar-looking, shapeless dark spot that seemed to shift in the air. I narrowed my gaze, wondering where I had seen it before and whether my ghostly apparition wasn't indeed a poltergeist or demon, and that's when I remembered the black fog on Cass's mirror in the bathroom when I visited her birthday party. That same day, my new vampire life began to fall apart. Had there been an entity in that bathroom? Did it follow me? But how? A terrible thought crossed my mind, making me feel hot and cold. Someone might have planted it there for my benefit—or doom. Someone had possibly meant for that thing to touch me. My brain kicked into motion, going through the list of people who attended the event. Everyone was there—everyone but the Shadows.

"If I told you a ghost was following me right now, would you believe me?" I whispered.

"Of course, I would. You're a necromancer." Devon's answer came quick, without a single doubt.

I nodded. "Thanks. Let's catch up later."

"Are you sure you don't want Deidre to recast your spell?"

I shook my head. "Ask me again in a week."

Without so much as a glance back, I took off up the driveway toward the gloomy mansion to lock myself inside my room and get some alone time to think. Devon's answer had been the way any normal person with knowledge of the paranormal would react. That Aidan kept pretending I didn't see a darn thing or that it wasn't dangerous seemed suspicious. It made countless alarm bells go off in my head, just like the fact that he seemed to have more knowledge of the various types of magic than Devon whose people actually practiced it. I couldn't help but wonder where that knowledge came from. Maybe there was more to the three courts and their ancient war than I knew. Maybe it had turned into a raging fire that savaged everyone in its way. I could feel someone had targeted me and pushed me right in the middle of this war. If only I knew the specifics as to how and why.

I barely reached my room on the first floor when a hunger pang washed over me, forcing me to my knees. I ground my teeth against the unnatural surge to pierce my fangs into something warm and soft. A cold shudder ran down my spine and bathed my back in sweat. My insides burned, my stomach felt as though it was on fire that spread through my body, and all I could think about was blood. I cringed and fought the urge to scream and smash my fists into the wall.

A soft hand touched my cheek. I peered up at the dark, shapeless form of an entity hovering in mid-air inches away from my face.

"What do you want?" I tried to whisper, but my voice barely found its way out of my throat.

Your body.

Your life.

I wasn't sure whether I indeed heard the words, or just imagined them.

"You can't have my life," I whispered bitterly. "Just look at me. I'm dead. A monster. I don't actually have one."

The shape began to shift in front of my eyes, turning from a shapeless heap into a female form. I glanced up the long, beautiful brocade dress to the pale, naked arms with skin smooth as alabaster. An emerald ring in a gold setting adorned her long fingers with blood red, razor sharp nails. It was a strange ring, one that I remembered spying before. But where? My eyes shifted over the smooth moss green stone to the gold setting with what looked like carved symbols. They seemed familiar too, but my mind just couldn't put two and two together. Defying the fog of hunger pulsing through me, I raised my gaze to her face, and gasped. At the back of my mind, the knowledge had been there all along.

Rebecca's ghost haunted this place, which was probably one of the reasons Aidan didn't want to acknowledge there was a ghost in the first place. Because he *knew*. My heart broke at the thought of the one I loved possibly loving someone else.

How did she escape her eternal punishment of reliving her death over and over again in Hell's second upper plane? It must've been the reaper's blood—or life essence, or whatever coursed through their veins—she gorged on right before she killed my brother. It probably granted her the ability to travel through the different dimensions even though she should've been bound to Distros forever. But how did she trick her way out of Hell altogether?

Her red lips curved into a sly smile. She opened her mouth to speak but no sound came out. Her forehead creased into an angry frown. Her nails tore into her flesh where she balled her hands into fists. As things stood, she was still just a ghost who could only communicate telepathically with the one carrying

Layla's prize. With no body, she couldn't return to her former, bloodthirsty self, meaning she also wielded no power over the living immortals, who couldn't see her on the physical plane. Basically, she was harmless and it maddened her.

I ignored her as I forced my body into an upright position and, fighting the nausea settling in the pit of my stomach, made my way downstairs to the library. A plan slowly took shape inside my head. I couldn't wait to get started and kick the psycho out of my life once and for all, but not before I got rid of the hunger nagging at me.

Tearing my sleeve away from my wrist, I bore my fangs into my skin and began to suck as fast as I could, pushing the ugly, slurping sound I made to the back of my mind.

* * *

I don't know how long I stood there in the middle of the library, drinking my own blood, but it was disgusting. And not even *pretty disgusting* like you'd call a friend who just told you they had ice cream and pickles for lunch. I felt utterly revolting. Somewhere behind me, I thought I heard a woman's crystalline laughter. Great, now the stupid ghost was having a laugh at my expense. I licked the two punctures and pulled my sleeve over the torn skin that would heal within less than an hour, then stood up from my crouching position.

It was already afternoon. The sun spilled through the large window, bathing the library in glaring brightness. Even though I freaked out at the thought of having a ghost nearby, I was too miffed to show it. Rebecca couldn't do anything, not without a body, so I had nothing to fear. Or did I?

Forcing my gaze to the wooden floor, I dashed for the desk, grabbed a pen and a notebook, and then headed for the backyard to enjoy the last days of the Scottish summer. I sat down on the bare grass a few feet from the rosebushes I loved, and tucked my legs beneath me as I focused on the notebook in my hands. Even though I knew I couldn't write down what went through my head, staring at the empty white paper helped me sort out my thoughts until a rough plan emerged.

One of my priorities was to find out what kind of magic Aidan had infused into the gate and the fence surrounding his property. Then I'd look into who mastered the ability to perform such magic. Was it someone Aidan knew or maybe even Aidan himself? And finally, I would investigate the whole witch thing. Who were they? Where did they live and what was their connection to the vampires and Shadows? I had no doubt that the mirror had a special meaning in all of this and that Angel was at the core of events. She always claimed she had no powers, but appearances can be deceiving.

I lay back on the grass and propped my hands under my head, squinting against the sun, pleased with myself. Slowly but steadily, I was beginning to believe that I was an even stronger trouble magnet than my brother and that was bound to say something because Dallas *couldn't* stay out of trouble for longer than five minutes. In my case, maybe it wasn't so much a compulsion than destiny. Maybe fate chose me to solve the riddle. I could only hope she didn't plan my demise in the process.

Chapter 21

Aidan didn't exaggerate when he said he'd be gone for a while. Alone, locked up in the library, I spent the late afternoon and early evening researching the various symbols I had glimpsed through the mirror, starting with the eye.

In ancient Egypt and still to this date, the eye represented divine protection from evil influences. In the concept of Kundalini, which was formed as a part of the yogic philosophy of ancient India, it stood for heightened conscious awareness and perception above and beyond the physical plane. I didn't know which of the two definitions applied, but I decided on a favorite right after I stumbled across a brief blog entry discussing the importance of the eye as a window to the soul and its association with the Third Eye or otherwise known as the sixth chakra. While I had no idea what a chakra was, the fact that it's known as the center of psychic powers such as clairvoyance, channeling, telepathy, and astral travel as the bridge to the spirit fascinated me.

I *Googled* each psychic ability one by one. Clairvoyance meant gaining information about an object, event or person from the past or future through visions. To me, that described a Seer. Cass's aunt, Patricia, was one and she belonged to the broader term of fallen angel.

Channeling was part of my ability of talking with the dead. Of course, since everyone called me a Necromancer, *talking* wasn't the only trick I could pull with a ghost, but letting them possess me in a freaky séance wasn't something I'd ever try out. I had been granted this ability by demi-goddess Layla when I won her stupid paranormal race that ruined my life. Was channeling something that demi-deities could do? I jotted down 'deity' and underlined it three times, then moved on to my next point.

The Shadows aka Shaman warriors could astral travel to perfection, which became obvious when they entered Hell to retrieve the Book of the Dead from Cass.

And last but not least telepathy, which instantly made me think of Aidan and his ability to get inside a mortal's head to influence their emotions. Granted, it wasn't exactly telepathy, but I figured it counted. As far as I knew Cass was the only supernatural with the uncanny ability to read everyone's mind.

My head threatened to burst from all the new information. Even though the lines were blurred, it was obvious supernaturals had various abilities that defined them. Leaving out the fallen angels, whose role wasn't clear to me, the three main courts remained: the Shadows, the vampires, and the demi-deities ruling the Lore court. Maybe the drawings on the wall were the key to winning the war for hierarchy that had been raging for centuries. But how was it all connected with Angel who, as far as I knew, had no abilities?

Engrossed in my thoughts, I barely noticed when the sun set over the Scottish Highlands and clouds darkened the evening sky. The temperature cooled down. I sat up and crossed my arms to keep warm although as a vampire I wasn't feeling the cold the way a mortal would.

"Babe?" Aidan's voice came from the hall. He must've completely slipped my mind. For a moment my breath caught in my throat, and I almost forgot about his plan to find the mirror so Rebecca could return to the land of the living.

The lights in the hall went on a second before the door opened and Aidan stepped in, wearing his bounty hunter gear. My mouth went dry at his sight. The way he reached me in two long strides and bent down to place a kiss on my lips—so confident, so natural—I thought my heart might just burst into a thousand pieces.

"I missed you," he whispered against my lips. His hands trailed down my shirt to my waist. I didn't manage to utter a single word, just nodded like an idiot in love, wondering why I couldn't just tell him I knew all about his little scheme before I slammed something over his head.

"Did you have a good day?" he continued, playing his role of loving boyfriend perfectly. I nodded again as I found myself wrapping my arms around his neck to draw him closer.

Don't do that, you moron, a voice screamed in my head. Ignoring it, I lifted my lips to meet his hungry mouth in a deep but tender kiss as hundreds of butterflies fluttered inside me.

"You're everything I ever wanted," Aidan whispered.

He tasted of honey, and smelled of warm summer nights and a soft breeze caressing the blossoming rosebushes. He was *home.*

I pulled back and moistened my lips, avoiding his impossibly blue gaze. He misunderstood my sudden albeit half-hearted attempt at putting some much needed distance between us. "I'm so sorry you had to spend the last few days alone. But I'm almost done now and, as promised, I have a surprise for you."

Last time we talked, he hadn't mentioned a surprise. I looked up, suspicion and fear creeping back into my heart. "Maybe another time. I'm kinda busy with my project."

Disappointment crossed his features and the tiniest hint of a frown creased his forehead. I fought the urge to touch his cheek and kiss it all away. This stupid bond made me do things, like cave in when I didn't want to.

"It wouldn't take long. Half an hour tops," he said.

Even though I knew I shouldn't trust the guy, he looked so hopeful, I just couldn't deny his wish. Hesitating, I nodded. "Just make it quick."

"Thanks." He helped me up to my feet and accompanied me back inside the house, still holding my hand. Under normal circumstances, his touch would've soothed my nerves, but today it did the opposite. My eyes scanned the area, unsure what to expect, as he guided me into the hall and closed his eyes, signaling me he was about to teleport.

I pulled my hand from his grasp and took a step back before he could drag me to some eternal dungeon from which there would be no escape. "Whoa, where are we going?"

He opened his eyes and raised his brows. "Relax. I wasn't going to kidnap you. I told you I have a surprise."

Why did he sound like the axe murderer ringing on the door in the middle of the night, asking the home-alone teenager if he could use the phone for some fake emergency?

"Uh—" I opened my mouth to speak as I willed my brain to come up with a great excuse why I couldn't leave the house. Expecting guests? Let's just say, we were in the middle of nowhere so no one ever lost their way to our door, let alone visit *willingly*. Pretend I couldn't miss something on TV? Wouldn't work after the invention of TiVo. I raised my chin, proud of my absolutely idiot-proof excuse. "Aidan, I'm not going out wearing this!" I pointed down the front of my shirt and jeans.

"What's wrong with your clothes?" he asked.

"Are you serious?" I rolled my eyes and walked past him up the stairs, already working on my next plan to fake the obligatory two-hour I-don't-know-what-to-wear tantrum every woman experiences before a date. I almost reached the upper stairs, when I felt Aidan's arm wrapping around my waist. His breath caressed my skin as he whispered, "You look gorgeous just the way you are. In fact, I wouldn't mind if you didn't wear anything at all." An instant later, everything turned black, the air vibrated around us, the telltale sense of nausea settled in the pit of my stomach, and then I knew I was somewhere else.

The darkness before my eyes lifted. The moon, a perfect semi circle, hid behind heavy rain clouds, but the light was enough to help me recognize the parking space, which led to the house perched on the cliffs overlooking the angry sea below. My first happy memories with Aidan invaded my mind.

We came here right after I started working for him. I remembered the car drive and how confident and easy-going he had seemed. At that time I was too naïve to question why he moved so quickly from barely exchanging a word with me to wanting to date me. I didn't know Aidan had watched me in London and planned my arrival in Scotland so he could protect me, get me to fall in love with him and win the supernatural race, all at the same time. That night in that same house, I had fallen for him. Plan accomplished. Now I wondered about the purpose of this second visit.

He was about to whack me.

Or worse, tonight was the night when Rebecca would be taking over my body.

Heck, for all I knew, he might be planning both.

I held back a shriek at the thought and fought the urge to turn around and get the hell out of here. But I figured if I wanted to escape, I had to be cleverer than that. What was the point in running anyway when he'd chase right after me? As a bounty hunter, he'd find me in the blink of an eye.

"Come on," Aidan said, grabbing my hand and pulling me behind him. Slight impatience became evident in his voice.

"I don't want to." I stood my ground. "Is that your surprise? Don't you remember you brought me here already a few weeks ago?"

"I know that." He pulled again. I didn't budge from the spot.

"Maybe another time. I like it here outside so much better anyway."

"Amber, what's wrong with you?" Aidan asked. "Just play along. You're ruining my surprise."

Yeah, I bet I ruined more than that. Like his future with his beloved, the detached house in the suburbs and the two point four children. I wanted to scream in his face that he could have all of that, just not at my expense, but I didn't. He pulled again and this time I followed because, as much as I valued my life, I knew I couldn't fight fate. The guy was everything I had. I loved him to bits. If he preferred someone else, then he should have the happiness he craved. I'd die for him because I couldn't bear to live without him.

We reached the house and he opened the door. "I didn't bother with a lock. Now that you know about our world, there's no need to pretend, right?" He laughed softly. "Besides, everyone crossing this threshold knows they're entering at their own peril." I swallowed past the lump in my throat. Talk about dropping hints. Aidan held out his hand. "Please, after you."

Sudden panic grabbed hold of me, threatening to choke me. I shook my head as I looked at him imploringly. "Aidan, I know what you feel. I really do. When you're in love you'd do anything to be with the other person, but I don't deserve this."

"What are you talking about? Of course you do. You've been—" He moistened his lips as he struggled to find the right words. "Please, I'm not good at this. I've never done it before, so I don't wanna mess it up."

I was convinced I understood him. He hadn't killed someone like me before, but he didn't want to mess up his chances of being with the psycho ex.

Aidan pushed me gently but firmly in front of him, through the entrance and down the narrow hall, ignoring my half-hearted protests. We stopped in front of the door to the living room, and he grabbed the handle. In slow motion, I watched my life roll before my eyes. I was about to die and the guy couldn't stop smiling. Was it so hard to pretend it pained him? Did it not sadden him? Not even a little?

My panic turned into a rage I hadn't felt in years. "I know what you're about to do. You're—" Aidan opened the door as I shouted "—killing me!"

And then my gaze fell on the beautiful living room that was now turned into the most stunning office I had ever seen with countless candles lining the floor in the shape of a heart. The flickering candles mirrored in the dark glass, as though they were dancing for us. A huge glass desk was set up near the floor-to-ceiling windows running across the entire wall. On top of it was a silver frame featuring a snapshot of Aidan and me. I instantly wanted to lift it up and place a big, fat kiss on it. But what enthralled me the most was the huge stony fireplace set up right in the middle of the room in which bright flames leapt greedily at dry logs, creating that crackling and popping sound of burning wood that I adored.

I stepped past Aidan into the room, my mind searching for answers as to how this could possibly fit in with my assumption that Aidan might be about to kill me.

"Kill you?" Aidan said, touching my upper arm gently. I turned to face him. "Amber, what are you talking about? I thought you'd be thrilled to have your own office. And since this is my favorite view in the world, it might help inspire you to fulfill your dreams." He shrugged, as though it was no biggie, but I knew it was. For once, I had to admit I had been wrong...and I couldn't be happier about it. He didn't spend his time away from me planning my demise but rather revamping this place so I'd feel comfortable. A surge of love rushed through me and I brushed a stray tear from the corner of my eye. My boyfriend wasn't about to dump me. Our relationship was going stronger than ever.

His raised eyebrows told me he was still waiting for an answer.

"I meant, *you're killing me!* This is breathtakingly beautiful." I pointed around the room. "I don't even know what to say, except thank you and I love you so much." I rose on my toes to plant a kiss on his lips. As usual, he had to meet me halfway.

"My girlfriend deserves the best, which is why Kieran and I made this for you. Of course it was mostly me since he's been busy hooking up with Patricia." Aidan walked over to the white leather sofas on the left side of the room and retrieved a gift bag, then handed it to me.

"What is it?" I asked, pulling out a large packet wrapped in red tissue with tiny silver hearts.

"Open it."

No need to tell me twice. I removed the wrapping carefully, making sure not to damage the paper so I could keep it forever, and peered at the pair of designer jeans I cherished so much because they really made my butt look awesome.

"You said how much you miss doing normal things like shopping and since you ruined your favorite pair jumping out of that window—" His voice trailed off. The tiniest trace of a blush covered his cheeks. He was so cute when he was embarrassed.

"Thank you. Again." I wrapped my arms around him and buried my face against his chest so he wouldn't see the shame in my eyes. I couldn't believe I almost ruined my chances with the most gorgeous guy in the world by turning into a suspicious nutter. I vowed never to doubt him again.

"Wanna try it on?" Aidan asked. "I got you the right size."

I looked at the label and groaned inwardly. The guy knew my *real* size? Why didn't I think of removing the labels before I started dating him? I had just committed a horrible beginner's mistake. According to Cosmo's dating advice, a boyfriend must never know the size you're wearing because men have great spatial visualization based on numbers, hence can easily picture sizes, which might just cancel out the more flattering result of being in love and seeing everything through pink-colored glasses. The plan is to tell him the usual supermodel size, add the very generous number two, and that's the answer he should be given upon inquiring about one's size, particularly if you don't have a killer body like my friends Clare and Sofia.

"Uh, yeah, they might be a tad too large," I said.

"Are you sure?"

I slapped his arm playfully. "Aidan, I know my body better than you do."

"You're right. I'll take them back and exchange them for whatever you want."

"Nah, it's okay. They're bound to get smaller after a couple of washes." He looked so horribly disappointed, I swallowed down the sudden lump in my throat. No lies between us. "Oh, toss it. You got the right size, I just don't want you to know it."

"Why?" A lazy smile spread across his lips. I stared at his tiny dimple I adored so much as he continued, "You're gorgeous. Everyone else's beauty pales in comparison to yours."

I wondered whether he meant it or just tried to please me.

"I mean every word," Aidan whispered, sensing my thoughts. Something flickered in his gaze—an all-consuming fire that burned just for me. He brushed my hair out of my eyes and cupped my face as he lowered his lips onto mine. I pulled him on the sofa and began unbuttoning his shirt. For the first time in my life I had no doubt I was doing the right thing.

Chapter 22

Aidan and I spent the night at the cottage, but we didn't get intimate straight away because he insisted on teleporting back to the house to get a few things, claiming he'd be back in five. I tapped my fingers against the cold leather of the sofa, anxiously awaiting his return. My whole body was on fire; even my scalp seemed to burn from so much tension. This was *the* moment I had been picturing over and over again in the last few weeks, and now that it had finally arrived it felt surreal. As though it wasn't happening to me but to someone else.

I draped myself over the sofa, propping my head up on my elbow, only to sit up a second later. What was I doing? I couldn't look seductive if my life depended on it, so I decided to go with the girl next-door look. *Be cute and funny, behave like it isn't a big deal.* I nodded enthusiastically at my own thoughts. Yeah, I could do that. Only too late did I notice Aidan had already returned with countless pillows and a blanket, and was regarding me amused as he pushed another log into the burning fire. I realized he hadn't bothered to put his shirt back on. My gaze lingered on his broad chest, smooth and perfect with clearly defined muscles he could only have acquired through lots of exercise. I wanted to bury one hand in his dark hair and let the other trail down his chest to feel, maybe even taste his skin. My tongue flicked over my lips in response, eager to fulfill my brain's suggestion.

"You look a little flustered. Are you okay?" Aidan asked with a smirk. Clearly, the guy knew he looked good and he had no intention to claim otherwise.

Heat rushed to my face, scorching my skin. Thank Goodness it was semi-dark and he might not catch it, but I knew I was kidding myself. Aidan sensed everything.

"Yeah. I was just removing lint from my top. It tends to bother me a lot," I said. "You'd think for the price I paid for it you'd actually get good quality."

Smiling, he ambled over, his blue gaze, now the color of dark sapphires, focused on me. My mouth went dry while my hands turned all clammy.

"Maybe we should teach your top a lesson for misbehaving. Let's get you out of it and buy a new one tomorrow." His voice came low and husky. I nodded and opened my mouth to offer my assistance but he didn't seem to need my help pulling my shirt over my head. My fingers trailed up and down his naked torso, my mind marveling at how strong he seemed. In the soft light, I could make out a few scars that had healed and faded but never disappeared. I meant to ask him about those when his hot mouth met mine and drew me into the sweetest and most breathtaking kiss I ever had. By the time he finished, my mind was reeling and I was seeing stars. Literally.

Outside the window, a million stars dotted the night sky. I had never seen so many in my life.

I sat up mesmerized and whispered, "You were right. This is the most beautiful view ever."

"Second most beautiful view. It could never compare with you," Aidan whispered, drawing a circle on my shoulder. A shiver of pleasure ran down my spine. I leaned back into him, wishing we could just merge into one being.

That's the moment I saw it for the first time: a tiny silver thread, sparkling like diamonds, enveloping Aidan and me. Drawing us together.

Bonded for life. Forever and beyond.

"I guess this is our proof," Aidan whispered. "We're officially in love. It sure took you an eternity to fall for my charm."

I smiled and wrapped my arms around him as I pulled him on top of me. "No, it didn't. I fell for you the moment I saw you. I was just really good at hiding it."

Chapter 23

Spending the night with Aidan felt so natural, so *right*. As our passionate kisses became more intense, our bodies moving in accord, I knew I had been wrong thinking my sudden bloodlust had anything to do with Aidan's magic. Whatever was happening to me was definitely not his fault. The magic infused gates didn't break the Shadows' ritual either. And finally, I realized even though turning into a vampire had never featured on my bucket list, as in Top 100 Things To Do Before I Die, it was actually a blessing rather than a curse because I'd get to be with the man of my dreams for the rest of my existence.

In the morning, when the first rays of the rising sun spilled through the windows, I knew I had to talk to him about my bloodlust but he looked so content I just couldn't spoil our first night together, and hopefully one of many more to come.

"You're perfect," Aidan whispered, wrapping his arms around my waist as he joined me at the window to watch the silent sea hundreds of feet below us.

Bright sunrays bounced off the crystal blue water. Seagulls circled the sky, their cries filling the air. Everything looked so peaceful and serene, the complete opposite of last night's high tide when the sea had hit the stony cliffs angrily, covering everything in a blanket of gray foam.

"Thank you. So are you." I snuggled against him and took a deep breath of his manly scent, wishing I could hold it forever. "Do you think we could come here more often?"

He laughed softly. "That's not up to me to decide, babe. It's your place now. If you invite me, I certainly won't say no."

"In that case you have a lifelong request to pop over as often as possible." I turned to meet his beautiful blue eyes fringed by dark lashes. I wanted to kiss him so badly it hurt, but I was barefoot and he was so impossibly tall I had to settle on tapping the tip of his nose with my finger. "It's a great responsibility, so don't take it lightly."

"I promise I won't," he said. "But are you sure you really want to extend a lifelong invitation to a *vampire*? He'll be able to cross your threshold any time he so desires. He could even teleport without your knowing and hide in the shadows to watch you because he can't get enough of your beauty. And finally, he might even decide to visit at the most inappropriate hours, such as during working hours, or when he feels he just can't take another second without you."

"Yeah, I think I want that." I nodded. "In fact, let's make it an invitation valid forever and beyond."

* * *

Like everything in life that's so beautiful it takes your breath away, our perfect time together came to an end quicker than I wanted. By noon we returned to the safety of Aidan's mansion. Last night's events still burned bright in my memory, making me feel all giddy and loved up, and even a bit shy. Aidan felt the same way not including the shy part because the guy knew no shame. He couldn't keep his hands off of me. It took us a while to reach his bedroom on the upper floor because we couldn't stop kissing and touching each other.

"I need to get back to the Lore court and finish this Layla assignment," Aidan said eventually.

I pouted. "I miss you already."

"Me too, babe." He pulled me into his bedroom and closed the door behind us. I honestly thought he changed his mind at the last minute so I dropped down on his brocade bed, ready to take off my clothes again. Unfortunately, Aidan stopped me. "I'd love to, but there's no time. There's something I've been meaning to tell you."

I pushed up on my elbows as I regarded him intently. What could possibly be more important than a roll in his clean and expensive sheets, which always smelled of musk and *him*? I could actually live in those.

"I haven't found Seth yet," Aidan started, sitting down next to me, interrupting my thoughts.

"You'll find him eventually."

Aidan shook his head. "You don't understand. Do you remember why Thrain couldn't find Sofia in Rio?"

I nodded, thinking back to our trip to Brazil not too long ago. "Her ex cast some sort of magic around her so the shape shifter couldn't track her down. But he did, eventually. Thrain's not even a professional. But you are, so I'm pretty sure you'll find him sooner or later." I leaned in for a kiss. He averted his gaze. I sighed and decided I might just give up right now because there was no point in trying to seduce him into bed. When broody Aidan was in his working mode, he was worse than the cute rabbit from the *Duracell* adverts that, once you inserted the batteries, couldn't be stopped for hours.

Aidan ran a hand through his hair, hesitating. "You know Cass asked me to help track Sofia down because Thrain couldn't get her scent. What I never told you is *how* I track down whatever I'm supposed to find."

"You use a GPS?"

"No." He grinned. "I have something much better." Fishing in his pocket, he retrieved a tiny object and placed it in my palm. Stunned, I peered down at the gold ring with an emerald stone in a marquise setting adorned with tiny leaves and flowers. It looked just like the ring on the ghost's finger.

Just like Rebecca's.

My laughter died in my throat.

"Witch's blood," Aidan explained. "It was infused into melted gold to create three rings that would track down everything, from objects to people, dead or alive."

My finger traced the stone as thick as a fingernail. I regarded him, horrified. "You killed a witch to get her blood?"

He shook his head. "I didn't. They gave it away in exchange for something else, but that's another story. Anyway, the power of the witch's blood is released through this emerald. The gold alone wouldn't work, and neither would the emerald. They build a symbiosis, just like the vampires and the witches have for years. This ring helped me find you in London. It's been in my possession for centuries, and never let me down. That is, until the Sofia incident, and now again."

For a few seconds, silence ensued between us while I tried to understand the meaning of his words. I resumed our conversation first. "Do you think Seth is using the same kind of magic as Gael and that's why you can't find him?"

"It's possible." He hesitated. "But the strange thing is, two days ago I found out Gael was at the shed in the woods. I could sense him. I just don't understand why I couldn't see him."

"How do you know it was Gael?"

"Remember the first time he was here to pick up Sofia a few weeks back?" he asked. I nodded. "I picked up his blood's scent. You know, I'm wondering what he's still doing here with Sofia gone."

"Did you say he's at the shed?" I raised my brows. "That's where I think Angel is."

"Your Shadow friend? What's she got to do with it?"

I tried to read his expression. Was he just pretending he didn't know about Angel's disappearance or was he indeed clueless? His mind remained blank as I pushed past his barrier and saw...yet more blankness. He had no idea what I was talking about.

"Stop that," Aidan said.

I ignored his comment. "Angel disappeared while under Shadow surveillance. A few days ago, right before you stormed off to Layla's gig for the first time—"

"I was summoned," he corrected.

I waved my hand. "Yeah, whatever. Anyway, I had a vision of Angel trying to get in here. Judging from her expression, she was pretty distressed. I thought we had the same vision because you just tuned out."

"I told you Layla summoned me. It wasn't really a matter of choice, Amber."

"Got that part," I muttered.

Aidan leaned in, suddenly suspicious. "Since when do you have visions? You're just a necromancer."

"*Just?*" I couldn't believe the cheek! "Well, as far as I remember I'm very popular. Everyone wants a piece of this." I wanted to point at myself but ended up pointing down my chest. Aidan's expression darkened.

"No one but me is getting a piece of *that*," he growled. "And having visions isn't part of your job description."

I moistened my lips as I tried to find a way to diffuse the situation. "It was just once or twice and it always involved your gates, so I'm assuming it's a vampire protection thingy. No biggie." I waved my hand in his face. His mistrust softened just a little bit...until it came back full force. I realized the guy would've made the perfect mother-in-law: prying and overbearing.

"Who told you about Angel's disappearance? And what were you looking for at the shed? You still haven't disclosed that bit of information."

"A friend told me." I shrugged. "And I went to the shed because I was looking for Angel." A frown crossed Aidan's forehead, and I knew he wouldn't drop it until he had his answer.

"Was it Devon?"

I shook my head. "I have other friends, you know."

"Who?"

The guy made me sound so unpopular. I rolled my eyes, irritated. "If you *must* know, it was Angel's boyfriend, Brendan." Aidan's face remained blank. "Doesn't ring a bell?" I smiled triumphantly. "Yeah, you probably don't know him."

"That's not what I'm thinking about." He got up and started pacing up and down the room. His sudden restlessness made me nervous. I tapped my fingers against my jeans as he asked, "What made you think you'd find Angel at the shed?"

I shrugged again. "Don't know. I can feel she's there."

"Just as I can feel Gael's presence." He stopped in front of me. His gaze bore into mine and his voice became a mere whisper. "Do you know what this means? They're both there. Gael must somehow be involved in her disappearance. That reminds me of Sofia. He whisked her away to Brazil to kill her and get hold of her powers."

"That's ridiculous. Angel has no special powers. I always thought Shadows were trained to cast a spell, perform the odd ritual, and astral travel." I scoffed even though Aidan's words left a bitter aftertaste in my mouth.

"How old is she?" Aidan asked.

"Seventeen." And that's when it dawned on me. "If she has any, they'll only manifest when she turns eighteen, meaning she's completely exposed to anyone trying to take advantage of her. We've got to find her." I leaned in to brush his hair out of his eyes, my gaze begging him to help me.

Aidan nodded. "We do because something's not right. It wouldn't hurt to find out who Angel really is and why Gael would need her."

"I have something that might help. Be right back." I signaled him to stay there, and dashed down the stairs to my bedroom to retrieve the tiny mirror. When I returned, Aidan hadn't moved from the spot. I smiled and squeezed the tiny mirror into his hand. His expression changed instantly.

"Where did you get this?" He turned the mirror in his hand to inspect it from all sides. His thumb rubbed over the irregular edge until I could see a tiny trail of blood where it cut into Aidan's skin. The red liquid spread across the surface and then disappeared leaving no trail behind—as though the mirror soaked it up. It was barely more than a drop, but it still managed to awaken something inside me. I bit my tongue hard and dug my nails into my skin until I felt the tiniest sensation of pain.

"Why, a mere thank-you would've sufficed." I slumped down on the bed, crossing my arms over my chest, so I could hide the red marks on my skin where my nails had cut in.

"You got me wrong. I'm extremely grateful because I've been looking for this for centuries." He grabbed my shoulders, forcing me to face him. "Do you know what this is?"

"A mirror?"

"It's a key," he explained. "There's four of them and, once combined, they're said to unlock the door to an unknown parallel dimension. Though, as far as I know, no one's ever been able to find all pieces, so no one knows where it leads to."

"A parallel dimension? My brother would have a field trip with this one."

Aidan smiled, but I could see he didn't get my joke. Even though Aidan tried to bond with Dallas, my brother couldn't get over the fact that I was basically living with Aidan mere weeks after meeting him. Needless to say, they tolerated the other but never really warmed up to each other.

I grabbed the mirror out of his hand and held it in mid-air as I inspected the ragged margin where it had been broken from another piece.

"When did you find it?" Aidan asked.

"A few days ago." I tapped a finger against my lips and prayed he wouldn't ask why I hadn't told him about it earlier, but as usual Aidan didn't get the hint.

"And it never occurred to you to tell me about it?"

"I thought it was just a mirror." It wasn't even a lie. I never really believed it had any special meaning...until I realized someone always lingered near the hut, guarding it, hiding something, maybe even searching for something they couldn't find— because I had it? But I couldn't share my thoughts with Aidan. He'd get mad, lock me up for the next twenty years and claim it was for my own safety. "There's something weird about it. If you hold it up in the light and illuminate the wall opposite the window, you'll see strange symbols, like carvings. I did some research."

"Of course you did," Aidan muttered. "Where else could you be than in the middle of the battlefield, looking to solve the one mystery that has half the paranormal world on the edge of their seats?"

I slapped his arm playfully. "Getting involved is my second name. Now listen! There's an eye hanging over a pyre. I thought it must've something to do with a Seer watching the trees or woods. Maybe it stands for the shed."

Aidan's expression made me stop mid-sentence. "You're right about the Seer part. But it's not the woods they're watching." He hesitated. His gaze scanned the floor as he probably considered whether to tell me more or change the subject.

"You're such a moron. I swear next time I know something you'll be the last person I'll tell."

"All right." He nodded. "You're right. I'm sorry, bad habit. The Seer is watching Morganefaire, which is a town of witches."

"Why would a Seer be watching a town?" Aidan shook his head, signaling he had no idea. "The witches of Morganefaire," I whispered, marveling at how grave my words sounded. "What's it like?"

"You'll see soon enough when we pay it a visit. It looks like Morganefaire's mark has been found. If the prophecy is right, the war between the three courts is about to begin." Something flickered in Aidan's eyes. At that time, I shrugged it off because I didn't know what Morganefaire really was. Besides, Aidan was a pessimist with a tendency toward exaggerating, like thinking a war was about to start tomorrow when it might not for thousands of years.

Let's just say, sitting in his bedroom with the first raindrops of the day falling against the windowsill, my puzzle was slowly starting to take shape. While I didn't understand the meaning of what was happening around us, I felt the magnitude of Aidan's last words and it sent chills down my spine.

Chapter 24

In the end, I decided to share with Aidan everything I knew...upon one condition: that he no longer kept secrets from me, except for birthday and Christmas gifts. We ended up arguing for almost an hour, but eventually he realized I had something he didn't have: a cunning mind. Well, he kind of called it 'the unfortunate inability to keep out of trouble' but I'm pretty sure deep inside he meant to say I had a cunning mind.

Hours must've passed since our return from the house on the cliffs. Dusk was falling on the tranquil woods, but we were still sitting on Aidan's bed, engrossed in our conversation.

"I need to go," he announced.

"The Lore court. I completely forgot you need to sign in with Layla."

His gaze shifted to the floor. His lips pressed into a grim line for a second, but it was enough to tell me he was avoiding an answer because he didn't want to lie to me. I had probably just given him a new lead and the guy was already trying to sneak his way out of our agreement.

"I'm coming with you. A deal's a deal." I raised my chin a notch, ready to battle it out if necessary, but he just nodded.

"We're not visiting the Lore court though."

"Didn't think you were," I said, grinning. "You're going back to the shed, aren't you? To test the mirror."

He nodded again. "I need to see the drawings. Why don't you wait downstairs while I get everything I need?"

"Like that burning whip thing you attacked me with? Yeah, don't you think it's about time you stopped pretending that thing doesn't exist?" I clicked my tongue. "Besides, I'm not going anywhere because I don't trust you won't just disappear and leave me behind."

"The thought never occurred to me but, now that you're mentioning it, it sounds tempting." He regarded me, amused. "I was actually talking about getting some chains from the basement. Since we're no longer keeping any secrets, care to tell me why you kicked in the door recently?"

Oh, shoot! I completely forgot I never fixed it. If I told him about my sudden bloodlust he'd freak out big time and he'd never let me join in his search. We didn't have time for Aidan's drama queen antics. "It's a long story. I'll wait in the living room while you get everything you need. Just hurry up." I dashed past him and slammed the door shut before he could resume his interrogation. If I got through the next thirty seconds, he'd fall into his usual work mode and forget all about the door for the time being. But Aidan would get back to it before the day was over, no doubt about that.

* * *

Wrapped around Aidan's chest and waist, the rusty chains with loops as thick as two fingers looked like they weighed a ton, but Aidan didn't even blink as we teleported behind a broad tree. The path leading straight up to the shed was about fifty feet to our right...through lots of bushes and scratchy thorns. Seriously, I couldn't lose yet another pair of jeans. And what did he need the chains for? Was he planning to tie me up so I wouldn't get in his way?

"Why didn't we just teleport up there? If you're so fond of hiking through some bushes, we could've gone for a trek *after* this is over. And why the weird chains? Are you planning on towing a car?" I whispered.

"I'm glad that you asked," Aidan said, smiling. "I want you to stay here and watch them."

I raised my brows. "The chains?"

"No, they're for Gael in case I find him. I'm talking about the bushes."

I opened my mouth to ask him whether he couldn't have a heart-to-heart with Gael like normal people, but he just disappeared. Well, if he thought I'd be pleased to wait in the bushes while he solved the mystery and reaped the metaphorical reward, he was in for a big surprise. I started up the path when my phone vibrated in my pocket. The caller showed Brendan.

"Hey," I whispered. "I think I have a bit of a lead on Angel. I just need to find out how to get to her."

"Really?" The line crackled a few times. Brendan's voice seemed to come from far away. "Where are you?"

"At that weird, paranormal shed in the woods," I said a bit louder so he'd hear me. "There's something about a mirror and the wall."

Something moved in the bushes to my right. I turned sharply in that direction and listened intently. My hearing picked up a regular heartbeat but it was too faint to belong to a grown-up. It was probably just a tiny animal scavenging for food, however, I took it as a reminder of the universe as to what usually happens in a slasher movie. Someone's lost in the woods, talking on the phone or trying to get better cell reception, and that's when bad things start to happen. Obviously, this wasn't the time and place for a conversation.

"We'll talk when I get back to the mansion," I said and disconnected the line, then switched off the phone just to be on the safe side.

I had three options: follow Aidan's command to wait for him, sneak up the path, or teleport. If I did the latter I might just interrupt something important and he'd be pissed. If I walked, Aidan might hear my approach and hinder me from joining in whatever he was doing up there. I didn't even consider my third option—listening to his command—because I wouldn't be bored to death while he had all the fun.

Teleporting it was. For a moment, I felt bad for not listening to him, but I couldn't let a man dictate my life. Besides, this new ability was tricky and I could really need some more practice. I closed my eyes and focused on the door outside the shed, imagining myself standing a few inches away from my target. The air shook around me and I was drawn into that scary sense of nothingness that always made my stomach turn. When I opened my eyes I realized I wasn't standing next to the door but in the middle of the room and Aidan was regarding me with a huge frown.

"You couldn't just for once do as I said."

I peered from him to the blood red drawings on the wall. They looked just like the ones I saw through the mirror, only he had added more detail. I was obviously interrupting something important. "Did you do that?" I pointed at the red chalk in his hand and then at the wall. "Can't believe you didn't tell me you could draw like that. Let me see!"

"Amber—" He drew a sharp breath but stepped aside. "Don't touch anything."

"Don't worry," I whispered as I peered from the beautifully drawn eye to the pyre and the people surrounding it. Most were women of all sizes and shapes, clad in what looked like short dresses and armor, with long hair reaching down to their waist. Among them were a few men, standing tall and proud, as though to guard something. One of them caught my eye and I almost choked on my breath. I knew that face: dark eyes, bronze skin stretched over high cheekbones, a tiny scar above his brow, and black hair—a tad too long, just like Aidan's—brushing the collar of his shirt.

"Is that—" I didn't dare say Blake's name for fear Aidan might not take it well. And sure enough his frown deepened. "I thought he was a vampire."

"He is," Aidan said. "But before he met Rebecca he was something else. No one needs to know, Amber. If his kind finds out, he'll be dead. And even though we're no longer friends, I wish him well."

I nodded, suddenly putting two and two together. "He told you about this all, didn't he? Because you were friends."

Aidan averted his gaze, but I didn't miss the tiny flicker of pain in his eyes. For the umpteenth time I felt bad because it was all my fault. If I didn't enter Aidan's life, he and Blake would still be best friends.

"I'm so sorry." My hand reached out to him and our fingers intertwined. A tiny spark of silver light wrapped around our hands like a shimmery cord. Seeing our bond gave me strength because it told me Fate wanted us to meet, but I vowed to keep my eyes open for Blake. Trying to kill me was wrong, but I understood his motives. Like Aidan, Blake was fiercely protective of his friends. He thought getting rid of me was the right thing to do.

"I forgot to tell you I found drops of blood right here. I'm not sure whether the blood was Angel's, but it was still fresh." I pointed around five feet from the drawing on the wall. Aidan knelt down and brushed his hand through the layer of dust covering the floor. I saw the tiny spot, barely larger than a fingernail, a moment before he did. My lips twitched. My tongue brushed over my sharp fangs as a pang of hunger washed over me, weakening me so much I almost dropped to my knees, ready to lick the blood off the ground.

Averting my gaze, I groaned, disgusted with myself. Aidan didn't even seem to notice. "It's fresh. Maybe a few days old."

"Someone was attacked." My voice sounded faint, alien in my ears. Aidan shot me a strange look over his shoulder and shook his head.

"In the case of a vampire attack, there'd be no blood at all. Not even a drop, unless he was a beginner. Everyone else, using a knife or any other weapon, would make a big mess. This something else."

"What do you mean?"

He didn't answer my question. In one swift motion, he bit his finger until he drew blood. I peered at it, horrified. My mouth went dry, my tongue stuck to the back of my throat. Aidan squeezed the puncture until a tiny drop of blood stained the ground. I felt a growl forming in my throat so I pried my gaze away from the delicious liquid, but it didn't help. I wanted to taste it so bad I dug my nails into my skin. My head reeled, my body felt weak, unwilling to listen to my brain's command to stop this madness and just be *normal*.

"It's not working," Aidan said. "I thought it would open the portal, but it didn't." He stood up from his crouching position and peered around him, as though the answer to his dilemma would magically appear. Needless to say, it didn't.

"I wish someone could just throw us a hint, any hint, at this point because we're running in circles." I didn't want to sound whiny but the hunger inside me was killing me. My whole body began to throb with pain. I needed blood so badly I even considered running outside so I could bite myself again just to ease the craving.

A soft wind blew in through the open door, carrying with it something I couldn't immediately pinpoint, and a tiny shiver ran through me. Even though it was quiet, I strained to listen, but it was too soft, coming from far away. "Do you hear that?" I whispered.

Aidan shook his head. I signaled him to keep quiet. There were voices—hundreds of them, speaking in languages I didn't understand—talking to me, telling me something.

"Amber?" Aidan's hand wrapped around my wrist. "You're cold as ice. Are you okay?"

I opened my mouth to reply but no sound came out of my throat. All I sought was to listen because I knew the voices wanted nothing from me—they just wished for me to understand. My mind went blank. Time seemed to stand still as I dived into those voices and let their words reach me, brush over me like a lover's gentle touch. I didn't know how much time passed, only that it was time to let them go because they had told me everything there was to know.

Blinking, I smiled ruefully and waved ever so slowly. "Goodbye, my friends." My whisper was so low I wasn't sure I had even spoken.

"You're freaking me out big time," Aidan said. I turned to face him and grabbed his hands, squeezing tight so he, too, would understand.

"They spoke to me. And they wanted me no harm."

He raised a brow. "Is this a necromancer thing?"

I nodded eagerly. "Yes, and it's great. I went about it all wrong. They're looking for people like me because they're lonely and they want to help. There's nothing to be afraid of because they'd never harm me."

"Really?" I saw in Aidan's wide eyes how freaked out he was, but I couldn't help the euphoria I was feeling. For weeks, I had feared the dead, avoiding encounters with souls, when I should've worked with them, let them help me.

"Yes. Look!" I bit my finger and squeezed a drop of blood on the same spot as Aidan did, fighting the faintness and craving washing over me at the metallic taste. For a moment, nothing happened, and then the ground shook beneath our feet. And then the air grew in density and began to shift in front of our eyes, moving to and fro like a giant fata morgana in the desert. I squinted to see through the opal curtain into the alternate dimension lying beyond, but could only make out a vast space of *nothingness.*

"Your blood is diluted by that of hundreds of others," a male voice said behind us. "In our world, it's worthless, Aidan. You should know that. Her blood, however, has not been stained yet." My head snapped back to the man standing a few feet away. I wondered where he came from, and then I realized I must've opened the gate to another dimension where he had been hiding.

"Gael," Aidan whispered, answering my unspoken question. "What are you doing here?"

The only time I ever met Gael was right before he almost killed Sofia in the ritual in the woods. I remembered him as tall, but shorter than Aidan, with light-brownish hair and prominent features, not memorable, and certainly not above average. Of course, at that time I also thought he was just a guy trying to steal a voodoo priestess's powers. Seeing him up-close, something felt definitely different about him. It was as if he had morphed into a powerful being.

"I noticed you looking for me the past few days," Gael said to Aidan, inching closer, a dangerous smile playing on his lips. "I've got to admit, I'm not pleased you joined Layla's side." I could feel Aidan's heart hammering in his chest, his eyes narrowing, confusion clearly etched on his face. Gael broke out in laughter, startling me. "What? You didn't realize I'm Seth?"

With new knowledge about what he really was, a shiver ran down my spine. How could I ever believe the guy was *ordinary*? There was nothing average about him. His eyes were too hard, too predatory like those of a watching eagle. His mouth, now curved into a fake smile, signaled the personality of someone who wouldn't hesitate to stab his own family in the back to get what he wanted. And then his eyes, brown with a yellow hue to them, reminding me of Layla. Why didn't Thrain or Sofia notice?

"Your sister, Layla, has a proposition for you," Aidan said.

"Proposition?" Gael laughed. "Big sis wants to kill me, so don't give me that crap about a proposition. But you don't care about my life or anyone else's. All you care about is saving your brethren."

Gael was only a few years older than I was. I wondered why he didn't just use the word 'friends' like any normal person in our century. Brethren sounded so *old-fashioned*. So paranormal. I peered at Aidan, waiting for him to assure Gael it wasn't so, but Aidan didn't even blink.

"What brethren?" I asked.

"The one he's been hiding from you, raising for centuries so he can win the war," Gael said. "Layla can't blame me for doing the same, which is why I have my own proposition for you. Let's join forces and win this war that is about to start."

"Is that true, Aidan?" My voice quivered. My mind was still processing Gael's claims. Was Aidan really trying to raise an army of undead to win the paranormal war? I shook my head in disbelief.

Aidan's gaze didn't leave Gael as he answered. "Don't listen to him. That was Rebecca's plan. Why were you hiding, Gael, and where's Angel?"

"I wasn't hiding, I was here all this time, right in front of you. You just couldn't see me. It's a rare ability. You could definitely use someone like me. And as for the girl, she never turned up to our agreed meeting so I don't know where she is."

"You're lying," I spat, not believing a word that came out of his mouth. He had to have her. After bringing shame to the Shadows by trying to kill Sofia, the Shadows had banished him forever. He stood no chance of finding a master there, so he had to kidnap Angel to teach him how to use his Shadow powers. I knew my theory was right and yet something told me he was telling the truth because Angel was only seventeen. She couldn't teach him anything. "I saw her in my vision. Someone was following her. If it wasn't you, then who was it?"

Tension settled between us. A vein began to throb across Gael's forehead. "You think I'm lying?"

The guy had a short temper and was capable of anything. Up until now I thought we were stronger. Finding out he was a demi-god, I no longer did. My mind switched off as I tried to step in front of Aidan to protect him. Unfortunately, Aidan seemed to have the same idea. His arm wrapped around me and pushed me back, placing himself in front of me and a possible danger.

"I'm not a liar but the future ruler of the Lore court," Gael hissed. "Pledge your alliance before it's too late."

Not only was he dangerous, he was also a nutcase. I wanted to shout, if he were the future ruler his mother wouldn't have made Layla her successor. Come to think of it, Layla had a few screws loose as well.

"You still haven't told us where Angel is," I said, eager to get back to the topic that really mattered.

"I told you, I don't have her," Gael said through gritted teeth. "Someone beat me to it."

I opened my mouth to speak when Aidan squeezed my hand, signaling me to keep quiet. "Why should we trust your word?"

"You don't have to," Gael said.

I yanked my hand out of Aidan's iron grip and took a step forward. "Give us something so we know you're telling the truth. Why did you want Angel?"

"Because she's my sister."

Aidan shook his head. "She's not your sister. Layla would never have let Angel live if she were. If you want us to trust you, you really need to tell us the truth."

The shed fell silent. I could see Gael's mind working, weighing up pros and cons, as he bit his lip, smirking. "And then we work together?"

Aidan's muscles tensed. He was a born and bred Scot. Lying wasn't in his nature. If he made a pact, you could be sure he'd stick to his word.

"Are you going against Layla?" Aidan asked. Gael nodded. "You understand if we join your side, you will never touch or harm my brethren?" I frowned at his second use of the word 'brethren' but didn't comment.

Gael nodded again. "Deal."

"What?" I hissed, gaping at him. "You can't be serious. Did something fry your brain?"

Aidan ignored me as he shook Gael's hand.

"Angel is Queen Deidre's intended vessel," Gael said. "She's been since her birth. They're just waiting for the right moment to do the ritual, which is a month from now, at Blue Moon. Without Angel's body, Deidre will die. I tried to kidnap Angel so the Shadows' queen would perish. Without their queen, there's no successor to the throne and their civilization will split up into smaller, weaker groups that will be easily slayed."

"Is that true?" I blinked several times as I realized the magnitude of the situation. Without Deidre, the Shadows would lose the battle and the vampires would win. No doubt Aidan would jump at this opportunity. I swallowed hard. The bad guy had just saved the girl's life, except that—

"Gael—Seth." I hesitated.

"Seth," he said. "It's the name my mother gave me. The name by which I shall forever be known and feared."

I nodded. "You didn't kidnap Angel, did you? Someone else did."

He bobbed his head in agreement. His lips curled into that irritating grin from before. "Told you. The questions you should ask yourself is who did it and why."

Chapter 25

I peered out the shed's window into the dense woods as the rising moon cast a silver light over the forest. Aidan and Gael slash Seth were standing near the south wall, next to the open portal, engrossed in solving the mystery that seemed to surround Angel's disappearance. After the trick he pulled on my friend, Sofia, I vowed to double-check every word that came out of Seth's mouth, but Aidan didn't seem particularly fazed.

I pulled Aidan aside and whispered as low as I could, "I don't like this."

"What choice do we have?" he mouthed back.

"In case you've forgotten, he tricked Kieran into finding the Blade of Sorrow for him so he could kill Sofia."

For a second, Aidan's expression clouded, as though he only now remembered what happened just a few weeks ago. And then his face hardened. "Look, I know Sofia's a friend, but I've got to think of you, my brother and the others first." I opened my mouth to ask who the others were when he cut me off. "If I had to choose between her life and yours—and I really hope I'll never have to make that choice—I wouldn't hesitate to protect my mate. You understand that, right?" I nodded, wide-eyed. The thought terrified me almost as much as the determination in his eyes. I had never seen Aidan like this, so hard, so unwavering, so *cold*. It scared the hell out of me because it made me realize the stories about him were true. There was a different side to him, the one that people feared, and I wasn't sure how to react to that side in case I ever got to see it.

He stroked my cheek gently. "Why don't you wait outside while I finish up here? I'll be with you in a second."

I nodded and headed out the shed's door into the night. The moment I closed the door behind me, I sensed something was different. Nothing stirred except for a gentle breeze and the swaying tops of the dark forest trees. The air smelled of wood and oncoming night, and—

Blood.

It was just the tiniest hint of metal, but enough to make my stomach growl and my hunger kick in. My tongue flicked over my sharp fangs as I sniffed the air, my heart pounding wildly.

Where was it coming from? I had to find the source, if only to take a tiny sip.

I shook my head, forcing my body to obey my brain's command. No drinking. No more losing control of myself.

"Aidan?" I called.

He opened the door and peered out. "What's wrong?"

"I smell blood."

His nostrils flared as he sniffed, then frowned. "I don't smell it. Are you okay?"

"You don't smell it?" I inhaled deeply, realizing the sweet, metallic scent was gone. Obviously, I had been imagining things.

"Maybe you should come back inside," Aidan said.

"No." I shot him a bright, fake smile. "I need some fresh air. Just don't take too long." He hesitated so I waved him off. He disappeared inside again but left the door ajar.

Something was seriously wrong with me, and the sooner I talked to someone the better. I knew I'd have to tell Aidan eventually, and I vowed to do so before sunrise, but right now I needed to confide in someone who wouldn't freak out immediately. I fished my phone out of my pocket and called Kieran. The line barely rang twice when a metallic whiff wafted past again, this time stronger than before. My stomach growled in response. A pang of pain ran through my body, cutting off my air supply for a brief second. Baring my fangs, I dropped my phone and crouched to the ground, scanning the area. The forest remained unnaturally quiet. Even the birds seemed to have deserted this place.

From the corner of my eye, I thought I caught something red swaying in the wind about two hundred feet to my right. I knew instantly the delicious smell was coming from that direction. My brain switched off a moment before my vampire instincts took over. Crazed by hunger, I dashed through the trees until I reached the spot, and stopped in mid-stride.

The red stain was a bloody handprint smeared across a tree trunk. My fingers brushed over the still fresh blood, and I licked them clean. What should've soothed the hunger inside me only managed to craze me more. I needed to feed. Desperately. My vision was already blurry and my body felt weak.

The leaves rustled behind me. My head snapped in that direction and a growl escaped my throat. A shapeless, black smudge appeared in the distance, taking shape as it inched closer. A pale woman floating a few inches over the ground, her beautiful red hair spread around her face like a halo, her thin dress unmoving in the strong breeze. After she appeared in Aidan's mansion and I got a good glimpse at her, I'd recognize that face anywhere.

Rebecca.

I squinted and crouched again as I listened for a heartbeat. There was none. She was definitely still dead. Either that or I was hallucinating, which I doubted. Only a few hours ago I would've been scared out of my mind, but not after the encounter with the spirits inside the shed, who helped me find Seth.

You should run.

Her voice sounded crystal clear, as though she had spoken the words out loud rather than in my head. I was surprised to find it quite pleasant. Her tone was friendly, even benevolent. It made me want to instantly trust her, even though I knew that had been the demise of many before me. She was and would always be a natural born killer.

"I'm not afraid of you," I hissed through gritted teeth. When another pang of hunger hit me somewhere in the pit of my stomach, my legs buckled under me and I dropped to my knees, clutching my stomach in pain.

Not of me, Rebecca said, pointing behind me. *Of him!*

A steady beat, like that of a drum, echoed in my ears. I shot a glance over my shoulder at the hooded figure I hadn't noticed before. Just like Rebecca, he was standing near the trees, watching me, but his face was veiled. He reached under his robe and retrieved a dagger with a blade as wide as three of my fingers, then raised the hand holding a dagger and pressed it against his other palm until a thin, dark red rivulet trickled down his arm to the ground. In that instant, a gust of wind blew in my direction, carrying the scent of blood.

I had to feed.

Any reasoning switched off as my vampire instincts took over. A deep growl escaped my throat.

Forgetting Rebecca, I leapt up from my crouching position and took off in his direction, jumping over the dense bushes and fallen twigs like a blood-crazed animal on the hunt. The hooded figure disappeared behind the trees, out of my vision, but I was determined to give chase. I dashed through the trees, away from Aidan and the safety of the shed. Low-hanging branches scratched my arms and legs. My heart beat so fast I thought my chest might just explode. The farther I went, the more the cool air lifted the fog inside my head. Eventually I slowed down to sniff the air. Without the scent of blood, reasoning returned. I peered behind me at the impenetrable woods, wondering how I could've possibly let my guard down like that and move away from the shed without telling Aidan.

I closed my eyes to teleport, but without blood my body was too weak to obey my brain's command. I spun around as I scanned the perimeter. No ghost around. Everything remained as quiet as a tomb. In the distance, I could make out a path. Was it the one that led to the shed? I didn't know so I decided to go back the way I came from when the sound of approaching footsteps got my attention. Ready to fight for my life, I turned around to peer into Brendan's face. I sighed, relieved to see him, knowing he'd help me.

"Something's wrong. We need to get away from here." My voice barely found its way out of my throat.

He just stared down at me, his face expressionless.

"Brendan?" I frowned, a sense of uneasiness washing over me. What was wrong with him? Then I saw his hand and the red mark on his palm. His cut was healing.

"I'm sorry," he said through gritted teeth. Beads of sweat formed on his forehead and rolled down his temples. He knelt down on the ground and tossed his head back. I peered in horror at the way his muscles and bones seemed to shift beneath his skin. A painful howl rippled through his chest, making me flinch.

"Are you okay?" I inched closer, reaching out without touching him. He clearly was in great pain, but I didn't realize what was going on until black hair began to grow from his skin. I took a few steps back, mortified. My breath caught in my throat. Brendan wasn't a Shadow, like he pretended. He was a werewolf, and probably the one that tried to have me for dinner at the shed.

Without so much as a glance back, I dashed through the trees toward the path, twigs and leaves crunching beneath my feet. My arms pushed through the bushes; my legs fought to run as fast as they could. For a whole minute, I even thought I'd make it to the shed, until I heard a growl behind me.

"Brendan! Don't kill her. We need her alive...for now," a female voice called out. My head reeled, my ears were ringing so loudly I wasn't sure whether the woman's voice had spoken the words out loud, or whether it was all in my head. But of one thing I was sure: the haunting hadn't been a coincidence. Whoever my pursuers were, I was probably part of a bigger plan.

I had been all along.

Marked for death.

Chapter 26

The freezing night air burned a hole in my lungs as I sprinted through the trees and dense bushes, ignoring the fear threatening to choke me. When I asked Devon whether he thought stupid was my middle name, someone should've told me that it actually was. My mother just forgot to add it on my birth certificate. How could I have fallen for such a cheap trick as a bit of blood was beyond me.

A ghost couldn't harm me. I could fight whatever was out there, but not a frigging werewolf that probably could snap my neck in half with those fangs. I had witnessed his unnatural speed and agility, and knew I didn't stand a chance. Not when I was weakened by my need for blood, making me unable to teleport far away from the howling beast chasing me.

My pursuers were nearby; I could hear their immortal breath in my ears. I could feel it on my skin.

Inside my head. That breath of death had been lingering on me for days, touching me, testing my sanity. Aidan claimed the house wasn't haunted, that the scratches on the floor and the blood on the walls weren't signs. That the haunting wasn't as scary as I made it out to be.

But I wasn't crazy.

The poltergeist hadn't been a figment of my imagination.

It had been Rebecca all along. Maybe she found me with the help of the witch's ring. Maybe her ghost clung onto me when I left Hell after Cass's birthday party, possessing me, messing with my head and making me do things I didn't want to. Like distrusting Aidan, kissing Devon, and drinking blood. She wanted me to find the mirror, or why else would I keep returning to the shed based on a 'voice' that told me Angel was there?

The puzzle pieces were slowly beginning to fit. But I had no time for thinking.

Panting, I pushed through the shrubs, daring a look back. The moon hid behind black clouds that promised a heavy shower in an hour or two. Unlike my pursuers, I was an inexperienced hunter on unknown terrain. Maybe once it started to rain, the water would wash away my trail and help me escape before I was lost and wouldn't find my way to safety.

I dared another glance back. The ominous shadows were closing in on me. In the darkness, I couldn't tell how many because my vision was slightly blurred, but I counted at least two.

I could make it.

Who was I kidding? Even if I outrun the werewolf, that crazy, dead Rebecca with her ring would find me wherever I hid. Even if I managed to escape this time, Rebecca was no natural ghost. She was a vampire who'd keep coming back until she fulfilled her mission.

In the unnatural silence, I could hear the rushing sound of water which only meant one thing...I was close. My breath came in ragged heaps as I pushed forward, harder, faster, the adrenaline in my veins keeping me going, until I reached the tiny waterfall hidden deep in the Highlands. The falls were nearly swallowed up by a thick layer of swirling fog, but the entire cliff face was illuminated by moonlight. From here, I knew it couldn't be more than a half hour trek, and I would finally arrive at the one place that would be my safe haven.

Aidan's mansion.

A twig snapped behind me, making me jump. I turned to look at my pursuers when I realized there weren't two but three: Rebecca's ghost floating next to the crouching werewolf reaching up to her chest, her pale hand wrapped in his fur as though she could really touch him; the third was a hooded person, tall with broad shoulders and a hood covering his face. Instinctively, I crouched and bared my fangs, ready to fight. The hooded guy lunged for me and held out his arm. My attention was captured by the object he was holding in his hand—a mirror shining unnaturally in the darkness. I had seen that mirror before in the Otherworld when I retrieved the Shadows' Book of the Dead.

As I stared at my reflection, unable to avert my gaze, I barely recognized myself. Mud and blood caked my pale skin. My once hazel eyes, now red and purple from hunger and pain, stared back at me. Dirty strands of hair hung limp over my gaunt face and hollow cheeks.

I jammed my fists into the ground as I fought to escape my own reflection, but I couldn't move. The air began to tremble. My heart filled with fear at the sudden darkness descending over me. I snapped my head to the side, trying in vain to avert my gaze from the mirror that seemed to suck me in. My mouth opened to scream, but the sound remained trapped in my throat.

From the corner of my eye, I noticed Rebecca's ghost inching closer. Something cold brushed my cheek a moment before a tremor shook my body. I could feel my soul trying to clutch to my mortal body as she entered me, pushing me aside, trying to possess me. Merge with me forever. My vision blurred, my will weakened. Strong waves of pain washed over me, cutting off my air supply. Eventually, a scream rippled through the air, and it took me a while to realize it was my own.

"Get away from the mirror. It's a trap!" a male voice shouted. I knew that much, and yet my body wouldn't obey my brain's command.

From the periphery of my mind, I was aware of my body straightening and marching forward to greet my hooded pursuer. His hand reached out to touch my cheek; his smooth voice whispered something that I didn't understand.

Praise for a job well done.

A tear slicked my cheek.

Aidan, I'm so sorry.

It all happened so fast. The hooded figure raised the mirror and held it in front of my face. Something began to suck me in, stronger, faster than before. My vision blurred until the woods gave way to white nothingness. In that nothingness I spied Angel, shivering in her jeans and shirt, dangling from chains. The icy air around her vibrated as something strong and invisible seeped out of her. Kundalini energy—I remembered the drawings on the wall and the eye watching the pyre and the people gathered around it, watching, waiting. Angel was trapped inside the mirror, and something was stealing her life energy.

Angel's eyes fluttered open, and for a moment I thought I saw recognition in them. And then they closed again and she winced visibly, as though in great pain.

Someone shoved me hard and I stumbled forward, landing on my knees. A shout cut through the night, followed by a growl. A moment later, a strong suction pulled me from the white nothingness back into the woods. Whatever happened broke the mirror's spell. Disoriented, I opened my eyes and realized the hooded guy had dropped the mirror to the ground. I peered around me at another man—my rescuer—standing a few feet away, drops of blood trickling from his wrist as he spoke in an ancient language. The earth seemed to tremble where his powerful blood touched the ground. The very air around him seemed to sizzle. But all I could think of was his—

Blood.

Not again. My mouth went instantly dry; my tongue stuck to the back of my throat. The sudden hunger savaged me, urged me to feed, but my legs couldn't move from the spot.

Rebecca's ghost disappeared, and so did the hooded figure previously holding the mirror. The werewolf circled us once more before he took off through the trees. But I knew he'd linger nearby just in case.

My rescuer inched closer and pushed his wrist to my mouth, his hand guiding the back of my head as he whispered, "Here, drink."

I protested. I couldn't. I didn't want to. Not now, not ever and definitely not from a human. I tried to get away from him but his iron grip held me close.

"You need to drink. It will be okay." He pressed his wrist against my parted lips. I could feel my self-control waning.

My mouth pressed against the open wound, sucking greedily. His blood tasted like nothing I ever tasted before: so sweet, so *wrong*. And yet I couldn't stop. Eventually, he pulled away and lifted my chin to face him. In the darkness, I recognized the golden skin stretched over high cheekbones, the tiny scar over his brow, and the dark, burning eyes I once trusted.

"Blake," I whispered. "I thought you wanted me dead." Like everyone else, it seemed.

He shook his head. "I'm sorry for what I did to you and Aidan. It was wrong of me to assume your death would stop the Prophecy of Morganefaire."

Although I still felt weak, his blood running through my veins made me feel connected to him. I could feel his turmoil, his desperation, his wish to right his wrong. His heart beat against mine as he covered my back with his cloak and scooped me up.

"It's okay." I smiled weakly. "I feel guilty for breaking up your friendship with Aidan."

"It was all my fault. I wasn't ready to welcome you in our midst. I wish I could make it right."

"You did. You just saved my life."

He shook his head. "Not yet." His gaze bore into mine, holding it. "Listen, Amber. The war has already begun and you're in great peril. You and Aidan need to return to Morganefaire as soon as possible. Tell him the prophecy is right and that his brethren are ready. I will be waiting there, counting on you. Do you understand?"

"I do," I said, even though I had no idea what he was talking about.

"Come on. Time to get you home before Aidan starts combing through the whole forest, looking for you."

With a last glance back to ensure we weren't being followed, he teleported us to Aidan's mansion. The air crackled. My stomach turned. A moment later, he sat me down on the ground next to the gates.

"You need to tell Aidan about the bloodlust. From now on only trust him and no one else. And don't worry about it. He'll help you learn to control it. Kieran was way worse than you when Rebecca turned him. We had to keep him caged up for a year." He laughed softly at his memories and I couldn't help but smile with him. Before I showed up they were family. They still were. I just had to bring them all back together.

"Thank you." I squeezed his arm.

"Be careful," Blake whispered before he disappeared.

I barely had time to take a deep breath when Aidan's voice rang through the night. "Amber?" Thudding footsteps raced toward me and strong arms grabbed me in a tight embrace. His scent tickled my nose, and I smiled because I was finally *home* again.

"Are you okay? I've been looking for you everywhere." His face inched closer to mine; his worried gaze swept over my dirty clothes and scratched face and hands. "Tell me what happened."

"Morganefaire," I whispered. "We need to leave now."

My eyes closed as I leaned my head against his chest and let him carry me into the safety of his fortress. For the first time in my life I knew that no matter how dark the road ahead might be, in a world of danger, deceit and magic, sharing everything with your soul mate is the one thing that might just keep you alive.

THE END... —FOR NOW

Printed in Great Britain
by Amazon.co.uk, Ltd.,
Marston Gate.